Murder

has

Consequences

I0628089

Pat McGrath Avery

Red Engine Press
Pittsburgh, PA

Library of Congress Control Number: 2014958208

ISBN: 978-1-943267-26-2

Formerly published under the title, *Consequence*

Red Engine Press
Pittsburgh, PA

Printed in the United States.

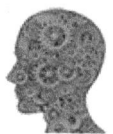

Dedicated to all who have been the victims
of greed, corruption and violence.

INTRODUCTION

I must say a word about fear. It is life's only true opponent. Only fear can defeat life.

Yann Martel, Life of Pi

SHE HAD COME here for the nuances of color, the quiet, and fewer people. However, today she planned to join the throng of gawkers waiting in line for their chance to see a priceless piece of art, probably the only antiquity many would ever see.

Why am I crazy enough to do this? I've had enough of crowds to last a lifetime. I've already seen it once. Michaela broke off her thoughts and turned up the radio. Johnny Cash stuck in Folsom Prison was better than the memories that threatened to paralyze her again.

Mick, who had worn the nickname from her earliest memory, pulled alongside the curb and decided to walk the few blocks to the museum. She needed to clear her head and a brisk walk worked well, especially when the salty Gulf air ruffled her hair and whispered in her ear. The breeze brought pleasure after yesterday's wind. She turned onto Queen Isabella Boulevard and halted at the sight of the block-long line. Fear ripped through her stomach and she reached for the support of a nearby building. As she tried to breathe in and out slowly, Mick grabbed her camera, holding on with a fierce belief that her new life would protect her.

Willing her heart to quit hammering the blood in her head, she reached into her bag for her panic pill. She slapped it in her mouth and gulped it down. Normally, she couldn't swallow it without water. The panic gulp worked even though she felt it stick to her throat or was that just her imagination? That precious little pill helped her survive an eternity of hell in the thirty minutes she waited before she reached the door.

The Treasures of the Gulf Museum was a tiny receptacle for such a coveted prize. The curator and Port Isabel city officials nearly burst their buttons when Belle Nueva offered to loan the Golden Booby statue to the museum for a year.

A couple of years ago Belle Nueva had come to Port Isabel in search of her missing grandfather who had retired here several years earlier. Belle had known he collected artifacts in his travels but she had no idea of the value of his favorite statue—a Golden Booby—until it was too late. Unfortunately some of his former colleagues had known far more.

Belle had found her grandfather but the fact was he had died, and not in his natural time.

How awful to have your body discovered in a parking lot behind a dumpster, she thought. No one deserved that. No, no one deserved to die at the hands of another, period. Mick blinked away her tears.

She paid her admission and stepped forward, marveling once again at how small the museum was.

The statue held a place of honor in the center of the front display room. When she'd visited before, she'd wondered why the curator chose the front room instead of one of the rooms in the back. After wandering around, she concluded that this room was the largest and probably the safest. Sometimes it's best to keep valuables in plain sight.

She found her spot in a quiet corner, prayed for security and waited for the wondrous moment when she'd feast her eyes on the nearly life-sized Golden Booby.

The crowd around the display thinned enough for Mick to see the statue. She searched for the unique aura she'd observed on her first visit but felt a twinge of disappointment. Maybe a piece of art only reached into the soul of the beholder the first time. She gazed at the statue, trying to get into the artist's mind. What possessed him—or her—to choose this odd-looking bird as a subject?

She memorized the lines and the contours, reveling in the vivid colors. She brought her camera to her eye. Not allowed to use flash, she adjusted the settings and focused on the statue. She snapped picture after picture, slowly sliding down until she sat on the floor. Good vertical options but she was smart enough to not try lateral shots.

If she stepped out of her corner, she'd never be able to hold the camera steady. For a few moments, she forgot her fears and lost herself in the exquisite beauty she saw through her camera's lens. She'd often pondered whether she saw or felt beauty—sometimes she swore she could smell it.

PROLOGUE

The larger crimes are apt to be the simpler, for the bigger the crime, the more obvious, as a rule, is the motive.

Arthur Conan Doyle

LESTER CURSED AS he drove away. If he hadn't listened to Fred, she would have died too. "The shot was clean. It's done," the man in the back seat spoke. Lester swerved around a car and seethed at the mistake he felt in his bones. If you take one person out, you're better off to take them both. He had tried to change Fred's orders but the man knew who was boss.

"You should have killed the girl too," his words came out through his gritted teeth.

"Just following orders. Fred pays me, not you."

"We'll be sorry. Did she see you?"

"No, it all happened too fast. She won't remember anything. I saw the look on her face."

"It's more than that. She knows why he died. If that leads back to us, you're in it too."

"All she knows right now is that a hole appeared between his eyes and he is gone. Nothing else will matter to her. Besides, as soon as Fred pays me the rest of my money, I'll be back in Mexico. You worry too much."

"If we go down, I'll make sure you'll go with us. I don't care whether you're here or there."

The man in the back seat fingered his gun. He'd love to blast Lester out of this world, but he might not get paid if he did. Better to bide his time.

1

When we are no longer able to change a situation—we are challenged to change ourselves.

Victor Frankl

MICK STARED AT her photos for the hundredth time. Why hadn't she realized that the statue she saw the first time was not the one she saw on her second visit? She'd felt the difference, but everyone knew that while hindsight may be right, it was worthless.

She looked at the headline from the year-old paper "Port Isabel Museum Curator Killed By Fake Golden Booby." Like most of the area's residents, she was still trying to absorb the news that Carol Flores' killer bashed her head in with a supposedly solid gold statue that shattered upon impact. Carol had discovered DL Casa attempting to steal the priceless artifact, and had given her life to protect it. Serving a life sentence in prison, DL now possessed neither gold nor freedom.

Could she have prevented a pointless death? She'd wrestled with that question for many nights. Sleep had given way to guilt. *I certainly know how to do guilt*, Mick thought. *I've excelled at it all my life but that solves nothing now.*

She grabbed her purse and jacket. She needed to get out of her condo but she knew she couldn't walk on an open sidewalk. She looked out the door, determined there was no one in sight and dashed for her car. She thanked the gods for the remote that unlocked the door.

She checked the back seat, slid in, locked the doors and fumbled with her seatbelt. She hated the shaking hands and wildly beating heart that translated into clumsiness.

By the time she fit the key into the ignition, she was shaking so badly she could barely turn it. She only ate fast food these days. She had been somewhat of a health nut before, but now she only ate where she could order at a drive-through. She knew she should go to the grocery store but she hadn't been able to make herself get out of her car when she'd tried.

Today she chose McDonald's. She couldn't face going back home so after she received her order she parked in the most secluded area of the parking lot. As she ate her unhealthy, overly salty burger and fries, she counted her blessings. She found comfort in knowing that good existed, even in her world without Matthew.

He'd been the best brother a girl could have—clueless to her needs but he had always listened to her, included her in his activities and tolerated her desire for privacy. He never understood her but then no one did.

How could they when even she didn't understand herself ?

Think of something else, Mick scolded herself. She picked up her iPad and browsed through her photos. Remembering the scene she tried to capture always took her mind back to the photo site. Her photos rarely captured the vivid colors of nature and the sunlight's true enhancement but reviewing them became a favorite way to relive the beauty.

Lost in thought, she stepped out of the car to dump her trash in the receptacle. She walked across the drive and, oblivious to her surroundings, she bumped into a rail and stumbled.

"Hello," a deep voice startled her. "Do you need help?"

She turned to see an older man with a kindly face, and a tomboyish young girl with an iPad in hand.

"No, I'm okay."

"You look pale."

"I'm fine." Mick hated the attention. Finding herself out in the open quickened her pulse. She glanced around. It took a minute for recognition to register in her brain. She'd met this man after last year's murder at the museum, but she couldn't recall his name. He'd worked with the police during the investigation.

"You weren't paying attention, were you?" The girl's inquisitive brown eyes and ready smile caught Mick's attention.

"No, I wasn't." Mick hoped that would end the conversation.

"I do that all the time. Do you live here?"

"No...yes, well, I moved down here last year." Mick felt her fingers tighten around her keys. She refused to encourage conversation but she didn't want to be rude either.

"I'm visiting with my dad. I love it here," the girl jabbered on.

"I have to go."

"We're headed to the beach. My name's Elena, by the way. What's yours?"

Mick started walking back to her car and pretended not to hear.

"Wow, Hap, I think we've been snubbed," Elena whispered.

I heard that but I don't want to talk to a happy kid right now, Mick told herself. *What does she know about life? She's probably never experienced fear... I'm being a jerk, the kind of person that made me feel small when I was her age.*

She turned back. "I'm sorry. I was thinking of something else and didn't hear what you said." It was only a partial lie.

"I'm Elena. What's your name?"

"Mick." No way would she give her real name to a stranger in an unwelcome conversation.

"That's a cool name."

Mick nodded and started walking again. Elena kept pace with her and the man walked a step behind. Surely the girl would soon realize that it was a one-way conversation.

"This is Hap," Elena waved her hand toward the man. "He's my friend."

Hap acknowledged the introduction and lapsed into silence again. Apparently he realized the girl talked enough for both of them. Mick thanked God that he didn't mention their past meeting.

"This is my second visit to South Padre Island."

Mick turned in time to catch Hap's smile. Obviously he was smitten with this girl's enthusiasm. Somehow, that warmed her.

Mick wondered if his kindly manner revealed his character. He hadn't said ten words but he watched over Elena. Surely he was an honorable man. Mick hated that she had to doubt someone's intentions.

Something about him fascinated her. She felt a stab of pain as she thought that Matthew's kind face would never age.

"What was your name again, sir?"

"Hap. Hap Lynch. I live here. Where did you come from?"

"Kansas City, Dallas, and several places before that." Not true, but good enough for this conversation.

"I drove through Kansas City recently when my wife and I visited Jefferson City. That's where I met Elena."

"I helped him solve a murder there." Excitement lit Elena's eyes.

Shock registered on Mick's face. She turned her head but couldn't hide it. "I...I'm sorry... I guess I wasn't prepared for that."

2

No one ever told me that grief felt so like fear.

C. S. Lewis, "A Grief Observed"

HAP RECOGNIZED MICHAELA from the from the museum murder investigation. More than her face, he remembered the nervousness and the fear.

"She's scared, isn't she?" Elena shook her head. "I won't ever let anything scare me like that."

"Ah, the confidence of youth." Hap needed to make a point. "You know the old Indian saying, 'Never judge a person until . . .'"

"I know, 'until you walk a mile in his shoes.' I wasn't judging her . . . well, not exactly . . . I was, wasn't I?"

Hap smiled.

"I promised myself I'd start making adult decisions now that I'm thirteen. It's harder than I thought," Elena said.

* * *

Betty gave in to lethargy and slept in. *Truth is, it's harder every morning to face another day.*

Her half-brother's arrest for murder last year changed her life. Until then, her mediocrity had been her private curse, but now it was public knowledge. The struggle to ignore the pitying glances from friends sapped every ounce of energy and then some.

She dozed again as the headlines burned in her brain:

Killer blames sister, assistant curator, for museum murder.

The whole sordid story came out. Her brother, DL Casa, used her to steal the Golden Booby, a priceless statue, from the museum where she worked as assistant curator. He called her stupid and wimpy, and admitted to the reporter that it had been too easy. He'd killed her friend. *He destroyed my life and he's the only family I have.*

Finally Betty bolted up in bed, or at least as close to bolting as she could at her age, and swung her feet to the floor. She was tired of feeling sorry for herself. She vowed she'd move forward with her life and hold her head up. She lived her whole life in the Rio Grande Valley and she wasn't going to leave. She wouldn't let him ruin her future, too.

She turned on a Neil Diamond CD, and dressed to memories of her youth. How she loved music! It had soothed her soul during many lonesome days and today would be no different. She cranked it up another notch and sang along to "Sweet Caroline."

She'd walk the beach today and let her senses revel in the sights, sounds and smells. She grabbed a breakfast bar and ate it while she loaded her beach bag with her sunscreen, shoes, a towel, iPod, and a couple bottles of water.

Two hours later she favored a sore knee as she stretched out on her beach towel. The hot sun warmed her tired muscles but she'd needed the long walk in the sand. She examined the one shell she'd picked up—a perfect sundial, not yet bleached out by the sun.

Drowsiness won the battle and Betty slipped into sleep.

"Ma'am, wake up."

Resentment flashed through Betty as she became aware of a voice.

"Leave me alone," she muttered.

"Ma'am, I'm sorry but your face and arms are really red. I think you've gotten a sunburn and I . . ."

Damn, Betty thought. Aloud she said, "I . . . I must have forgotten to put on more sunscreen." *How can I be so stupid? I'm as pathetic as DL told everyone.*

"Oh, look. You found a sundial. That's awesome!" Betty looked up into the face of a young girl.

She has kind eyes. God, I'm pitiful. I'm so desperately searching for kindness.

"May I see it?" The girl ignored Betty's lack of response. "I'm Elena, by the way. I'm here on vacation."

Betty handed her the shell. "Yes, I picked it up today."

"I love the symmetry of sundials. Actually, I love all kinds of shells and it's amazing to think of the creatures that live in them. Don't you think so?"

Betty shook her head and wished the girl would leave her alone. No, that wasn't true. She wanted her to talk forever but not ask for any response. She needed to hear another human voice. She looked at her reddened arms and reached for the sunscreen in her bag.

"Here, do you need help?" the girl asked.

"No, I'm fine."

"Okay. I didn't mean to bother you. I just wanted to help . . . I'll leave you alone." The girl turned away.

"No, don't go. I . . . I'm not fully awake yet. What did you say your name is?"

"Elena Reyes. What's yours?"

"Betty."

"Do you live here?"

"Yes."

"If I lived here, I'd be on the beach every day. I love the smells, the sounds, and all the sights. Don't you?"

"Yes."

"Do you live on the island?"

"No." Betty finished applying the sunscreen, snapped the lid shut and placed it back in her bag. "Port Isabel."

"I like Port Isabel, too, especially the lighthouse and all the ghost stories . . . Well, I have to go. My friend will be waiting for me. I hope you don't have a bad sunburn."

"It won't be. Thanks for waking me."

* * *

After the girl left, Betty squinted against the basketball-sized sunspots cast by the blazing sun. She turned west in time to catch a great blue heron flapping its wings and pushing off into flight. The loneliness of the dunes dulled the sounds of the waves behind her.

God, I need a friend, she swallowed back the moan that almost escaped.

She watched a seagull peck a hole in a sand dollar. "Will you spend some time with me, little guy?"

The bird skittered away, leaving nothing but footprints behind.

Betty stooped to pick up a shell, blinking back the tears that threatened. She had forced herself out of bed, hoping a morning on the beach would lift the grey fog that crushed her. She hadn't taken time for a cup of coffee. Maybe it was just the lack of caffeine.

The aloneness she once craved had turned into a loneliness that smothered her. Uncle Robert had disappeared last year and her newly found half-brother had a new home in the state prison. The idea of prison didn't bother her but his cruel betrayal still hacked away at her self-esteem. "She's a wimpy old gal and a bore." That's how he had described her.

"Good morning."

Betty straightened up and looked into the eyes of an attractive, smiling thirty-something woman.

"Hello," Betty tried to blink away her unshed tears.

"Are you all right?"

"I'm fine." Obviously the blinking hadn't worked. *God, make her go away,* she prayed.

"Did you find any shells?"

"Huh . . . ? Oh, no, I wasn't looking." What a fool thing to say. She'd been picking up a shell when the woman spoke to her.

"You look familiar. I'm trying to place where I've seen you."

"Probably around town."

"I'm Maria. My brother lives on the island. His name is Roberto. Do you know him? Roberto Rodriguez-Garcia."

Betty felt the blood drain from her face. *Please, God, don't let me faint.* The memories slashed through her. "I've heard the name," she settled on a half-truth. "I need to go. I'm not feeling well."

"Nice to meet you. Hope you feel better," the woman smiled and left.

In her car, Betty gripped the steering wheel. She needed to stop shaking. Roberto. He had been Carol's new friend, the one she kept secret. Now Carol was dead and she didn't want to think about her. If she had only stayed later that day, Carol might still be alive. She had died for nothing and it had been Betty's newfound half-brother who had killed her.

3

**The mind is everything. What you think
you become.**

Buddha

LESTER SEARCHED THE Internet as he did
every evening. Michaela Riley. He had to find
the bitch and take care of her.

A knock on the door broke his concentration.

"What do ya want?" He growled as Fred, the
stupid idiot who created this whole situation,
walked in the room. If he'd taken care of business
in the beginning, Michaela wouldn't be an issue.

"We've got a meeting tonight. Are you ready?"

"Yeah, and you'd better not screw it up this time."

"Hey, I didn't screw anything up." Fred looked at
the dirty dishes and empty bottles. His nostrils
flared at the stench of stale cigarettes and alcohol.
Lester was a slob.

"Then why do we have to worry about that bitch?"

Lester hated the way Fred thought he was too good to get his hands dirty. He should have taken care of things himself.

"We don't. She doesn't know anything and never did. The problem ended with Matthew. You worry for nothing."

Lester gripped the pistol in his pocket. He'd love to put a bullet right through Fred's arrogant smirk. Fred may be smart and well dressed but he was stupid when it came to people. Lester had street smarts and he knew it. That sense told him that Michaela was a threat as long as she was alive.

He didn't know if Matthew had told her about the business but he knew that any potential witness could topple their little empire. He wasn't about to allow that to happen. It had taken him years to set up his distribution system, bribe the Border Patrol agents, and build a team he could trust. Fred thought he was the business genius but Lester knew how to build his organization one step at a time. No bitch would knock it down.

"I won't rest as long as she's alive," he spit out to himself as much as to Fred.

Fred changed the subject. "What about tonight's shipment? That's what I came by to talk about. Is everything in place?"

"Yes, we're clear as long as the truck leaves the border before two. If that new agent shows up early, he could create problems. How many do we have?"

"A full truckload. You'll be at the farm when the truck arrives?"

"Don't worry, I'll be there."

Fred nodded and walked to the door. He hoped Lester would lay off the booze but it wouldn't do any good to remind him. As long as Lester thought he was in charge, Fred knew how to manipulate him. He also knew never to chastise him about his drinking or slovenly ways.

They'd created a gold mine and both of them knew it. They were unlikely partners but they needed each other. Fred had the class and social skills to negotiate deals. Lester had a quick temper and a belief that brute force topped brains any day. However, Fred recognized Lester's cleverness and innate ability to solve problems.

Matthew Riley had been the third partner but he'd balked at their project's human cost. Lester had been right to get rid of him. He just handled it publicly and poorly. He'd have to control him better in the future.

* * *

Fred, Frederick to his employees at the bank, disliked Lester with a passion hard to hide. The guy made him feel dirty, like the grit that gets under your fingernails and in your nostrils. There was a stench to crass and he smelled it on Lester.

Their business venture made money, loads of it. He wanted to run it with class since he couldn't do so legally. One commodity was the same as the next, wasn't it? Fred had made it the hard way and he wasn't about to return to the insecurity he'd lived through in his youth.

He had abhorred the weekly visits to church, the daily prayers thanking God for all His gifts and the constant moralizing from his parents. It never made sense when they spent the rest of the time struggling to keep their home and pay their bills. He wasn't planning to have God take care of him. He knew he was on his own.

Besides, he stayed away from the bad stuff. He didn't run a prostitution or white-slavery operation. He kept it clean. Whatever happened later was none of his business. He was simply in the logistics end of the business.

Fred didn't worry about Michaela. Matthew would never have endangered his cash cow. He regretted losing Matthew but "getting religion" had made him dangerous. *You never take chances and Matthew had become a risk*, Fred rationalized. Now he had to keep tight control over Lester.

* * *

Mick checked the other car in the parking lot. Even in a small place like Paragraphs, she never felt secure. Only one car meant that the bookstore should be safe. She loved hanging out with books and gabbing with Griff and Joni, the owners. She grabbed the cards from the back seat, checked the parking lot one more time and hurried into the store.

"Michaela, welcome to Paragraphs this beautiful morning," Griff 's smile required one in return.

I miss the smiles that used to come so readily, Mick realized. Matthew had a brilliant smile, the kind that casts its brilliance on everyone around him. She learned to smile from him.

"Hi, I brought some of my card prints for you," Mick handed them to him as she scanned the store for the other customer.

"Looking for someone?" Griff asked.

He knows I'm afraid but what can I say? Mick thought.

"You know Hap Lynch and Elena Reyes, don't you? They are out in the courtyard. I think Hap is napping while Elena reads."

"Yes and no. I've met them but don't really know them." Mick wished she could relax her neck muscles. She straightened her shoulders and glanced at the door. She felt safer, just a smidgeon but she didn't want to talk to anyone else.

"I love the cards. You cast our beautiful island in a brilliant light." Griff smiled.

"Thanks." After they conducted their business, Mick browsed through the books about the island. She found herself relaxing her guard and that frightened her. The possibility of discovery shadowed everything and she needed to remember that. She had to get out of here, get home and lock the doors.

"I've got to go," she mumbled to herself.

"I heard that," Griff laughed. "Don't you want to say hello to Hap and Elena first? She's getting restless out there and that means she'll be bursting through the door any second."

"No, not now." Mick knocked a book on the floor in her clumsy effort to hurry. She stooped to pick it up as the acrid taste of panic filled her throat. By the time she fumbled with her car keys, jumped in and locked the door, she could no longer control the shaking. She swiped at her tears with the back of her hand and gulped for air. Maybe if she could remember that day, she could control the fear.

Maybe she needed a psychiatrist so she could talk to someone. If only she had a friend, but Mick knew she could never put a friend in danger. No, her life was aloneness, for how long she didn't know. There was no statute of limitations on murder. Would she have to live the rest of her life alone? The tears flowed as painful sobs racked her body.

"Hello in there," the voice and knock on the window startled her. Why the hell couldn't people leave her alone?

"Hello," the voice called again when Mick didn't turn her head. "Are you all right? May I help?"

Mick swallowed a sob, blotted her eyes with a McDonald's napkin that she'd left on the seat, and turned to look at the Good Samaritan. "I . . . I'm fine." *Please leave. I can't talk to anyone right now.* She'd seen that woman before but where? She had one of those forgettable faces that could easily get lost in a crowd. She would never have to worry about someone finding her because she'd always melt into the woodwork. *Where have I seen her? Think.*

"Are you sure you're all right? Is there something I can do?"

Why doesn't the stupid woman go away? Can't she see I don't want to talk?

"I feel like I should know you," the woman babbled. "Where might I have seen you before? Do you live here?"

Mick's horizontal headshake should have been enough of an answer but that wasn't stopping this busybody.

"My name is Betty. I live in Port Isabel. I used to work at the museum . . . that's it. You visited the museum when. . . . Oh my God, I've got to go. I hope you're all right." Betty turned and hurried into Paragraphs.

God, I need a friend, Mick swallowed back the moan that almost escaped. She backed out of her parking space, slammed her car into drive, and turned right out of the parking lot without looking either direction.

I've got to get control of myself. I can't spend my entire life in my condo. Maybe South Padre Island wasn't far enough away or maybe it was the small-town friendliness. Mick knew she might have to move. Did everyone recognize her? Being remembered was a curse. She'd dyed her hair and let it grow long. She'd changed her clothing style and chosen a darker makeup base. After also changing her last name, she hoped Matthew's murderer wouldn't recognize her now.

After she'd made it home and locked herself in her condo, she opened her computer and brought up Google Earth. Where could she go?

4

Evil men by their own nature cannot ever prosper.

Euripides

MICK STOPPED MATTHEW to ogle the spectacular colors created by the light's reflection on the angled glass overhang. Out of the corner of her eye she saw the car speed close to the curb. She caught sight of the gun as she turned toward Matthew. She watched his smile disappear as a hole appeared between his eyes. His face blanched and blood dripped down his nose. He sank to the sidewalk, like satin cloth sliding off a table. Horror robbed Mick of her senses. Colors, light, blood. She screamed.

Mick awoke sobbing and drenched in sweat. It was the same dream that had wrecked her sleep dozens of nights. The same fear and panic. The same expression on Matthew's face. She sat up, wrapped her arms across her chest and rocked back and forth in the bed.

"I never saw the shooter," Mick had told the detectives who questioned her. In truth, she remembered nothing but the surprised look on Matthew's face before he crumpled to the ground. She couldn't identify the car and she never saw its passengers. The gun and the hole in Matthew's head—that was her only memory of that night.

She remembered nothing of the funeral plans or the service. She remained unaware of her friends' efforts to help. Everything had been a blur except she knew she had to hide. After the funeral, she'd packed up her clothes, closed her bank account, and spent hours selecting a remote location. She had to leave Arizona. Mick sensed danger even though she repeatedly admitted she saw nothing.

After she left, she read that the police determined Matthew had been the victim of a random drive-by shooting. Mick knew there was nothing random about it. After more than a year of running, the fear still consumed her. Everything had changed with that one shot.

Matthew had been her only family. Their mother died of breast cancer when Mick was ten and they'd lost their dad in a car wreck while she was in college. Matthew was the anchor in her life and she found it impossible to accept that he had been ripped away.

* * *

The truck rumbled down the dirt driveway to the farm. Even from the barn, Lester could identify the full load by the pull of the engine. Although he loved the thought of the money he'd soon have in hand, he hated the process he'd have to endure to get it. He needed a quick drink.

When the truck ground to a stop just yards from the barn door, Juan opened the door and jumped from the driver's seat.

"I'm here, Boss." Juan's loud whisper seemed magnified by the wind.

"Everything go okay?"

"Just like you said. No new guard tonight. Timing was perfect."

"And the load?"

"Full." Anger shot through Juan at Lester's casual reference but his face registered no emotion.

"Get Hank out of the truck and let's get busy, then."

Juan opened the truck's passenger door. "Come on. Let's get it done."

"Everything okay?"

Juan nodded and headed toward the back of the truck. He understood Hank's concern. The last time the two of them had experienced Lester's short temper for moving too slow.

He hated this part. Opening the door, smelling the waste and the fear, demanding the money and then sending a truck load of illegals out into the wild seemed like the worst form of cruelty. I've done a lot of things, he admitted to himself, but this is the worst. I'm throwing away my own people. They don't stand a chance in Arizona.

Lester's assurances had seemed so logical at the time. "You're giving them a chance, Juan. They will come anyway. We are helping them by getting them this far across the border." Now he knew it for what it was, a way for Lester to get rich. Juan knew Lester had partners but he'd never heard names. His job was to drive the truck. He no longer asked questions or wanted answers.

Juan attended Mass with his family every Sunday morning. While they prayed, he sat in fear of God striking him dead for this evil work. Funny how proud his wife was now that he brought home more money.

"Hurry up," Lester hissed. "Get the door open and get them into the barn." Making quick work of the padlock, Juan opened the doors. Noise and the stench assaulted his senses. *Pull yourself together man. It's a job*, he reminded himself.

Juan and Hank unloaded enough boxes to make a pathway to the partition. He opened the short, narrow doorway.

"Get down one at a time, go through that barn door and sit on the floor. Coyote will tell you what to do," Juan pointed as he gave instructions. He grimaced at Lester's name for himself. Juan failed to understand Lester's reference and thought it was just one more strange thing about his boss. "I'm just using the name for smugglers," Lester had said.

"Carlos fainted," a man held a young boy at his side.

"You'll have to carry him then, and he still pays," Juan said. He pointed to Hank, "This man will help you. Move as quickly and quietly as possible. You all have to be on your way before daylight."

"Have you told them to have their money ready?" Lester asked. He wished he could speak Spanish but he didn't care enough to learn. That's why he hired guys like Juan. Lester recognized his vulnerability.

5

Man is the only kind of varmint sets his own trap, baits it, then steps in it.

John Steinbeck, Sweet Thursday

THE MERCHANDISE HAS arrived. Safe. Fred sighed at Lester's text.

Price?

$3,500 each.

Will pick up as usual. Fred counted the money Lester gave him. $105,000. Not bad for providing transportation, IDs and drivers' licenses to thirty people.

"You know guys are renting passports too?" Lester thought it was one more way to expand business.

"Yes, but we don't want to muddy the waters . . . take chances. We have a system that works. We'll stick with it."

"Why miss out on an opportunity? We get the passports, we rent them before the illegals get to the border stations and then we get them back. Sounds foolproof to me."

"Drop it. Now, here's the $5,000 for Juan and Hank. Take care of it. How much do you need for the others?"

"$20,000 should do it. I need my split now," Lester said. "Here's your $20,000."

"I deserve more," Lester said.

"We've been through this before. We have expenses." Lester seethed but knew this wasn't the time to demand.

Fred refused to tell him what the "expenses" were. *I do all the work and he gets most of the money,* Lester told himself. *Things have to change.*

"When's the next shipment?"

Next Tuesday," Fred said. "I'll be in touch."

After Lester left, Fred noticed two empty whiskey bottles tossed behind a bale of hay. Damn him. One more thing to worry about.

* * *

Juan watched Jorge across the kitchen table, marveling at his son's innocent and intelligent features. Seven years old . . . about the same as the boy in last night's delivery. His heart hurt at the thought of the boy's future. If he survived, his opportunities would always be limited by his illegal status. Drugs and smuggling would most likely be his only career choices.

"Papá," Rosita nudged him. "I want pink shoes for my birthday party."

"Well, we will certainly have to go shopping," Juan smiled at his darling daughter. "Papá will make sure you have the prettiest shoes at the party."

"Thank you, Papá. I love you this much." Rosita spread her small arms wide.

"And I love you this much more," he teased as he spread his arms.

He lived to provide for Jorge and Rosita. Lourdes, his beautiful wife, loved the money but would give him a tongue-lashing if she knew how he earned it. Driving a truck was one thing but smuggling illegals was another. She might even leave and take the children. He could never let her find out.

"Why do you spoil her, Papá? She's already a brat," Jorge complained.

"Ah, Jorge, I spoil you both. I want you to have a good life."

"We do, Papá."

"We do, Papá," Rosita echoed her big brother.

Later when the children were asleep, Juan still saw the young boy's face. His father cared for him as he cared for Jorge and Rosita.

"I've never understood why some of us are lucky and some have no luck," he muttered.

"Did you say something," Lourdes asked from the doorway.

"Nothing."

"It's bedtime," she said.

* * *

"Wait a minute. Do you ever wonder why some people never seem to get any breaks? Why we're so lucky?"

"God looks after us, that's why."

"But why doesn't He look after everyone?"

"I don't know, Juan. I'm tired. Just be thankful He takes care of us."

Sleep didn't come to Juan. He spent the night haunted by a young boy's face and questions for which he found no answers. He saw no need to pray because he couldn't cope with God's anger. At least my family is happy with the money, he told himself.

6

**We must let go of the life we have planned,
so as to accept the one that is waiting for us.**

Joseph Campbell

"DO YOU EVER worry about people, Hap?"
Elena's expression spoke volumes.

"Are we talking about a specific person or people
in general?"

"Mick. When I met her, she seemed unhappy and
scared. Yesterday, Griff said she was in the store
and she didn't even speak to us after he told her
we were there. I think something's wrong."

"I agree that she's unhappy and scared but she
may have had a good reason for not taking time
to visit with us yesterday. I do suspect something
is frightening her. Until she's ready to confide
in us, I don't think we can help though."

"I can still worry about her."

"Elena, you've got a good heart but worry doesn't solve anything. It's one of the things we have to learn in life. We can't solve someone else's problems."

"I know that. I keep trying to get Mom and Dad back together but it never works. I'm beginning to realize they have to solve their own problems."

"It's a tough lesson when you learn your parents aren't perfect. They're just people trying to live their lives the best they can and not hurt you in the process." Hap had met her mom and dad. They both seemed like good people but who knew why marriage worked for some and not for others. Being nice people didn't solve problems.

"Yeah, I went through all that kid stuff of blaming myself, but I've gotten over that. I still want them to get back together but I don't think they will – at least not for a while. But that's different than seeing someone as scared as Mick. I still have to worry about her."

"I know. Me too." Hap realized he might as well admit the truth.

"Will you try to talk to her, Hap? Please."

"Let's give her a little longer first. Maybe she'll ask for help."

"She won't. Please!"

"Okay, when the opportunity presents itself."

* * *

Mick didn't leave her house for the next two days. It was the safest place in her world. Sure, she had to check the doors and the windows every couple of hours to make sure they were still locked and secure. She longed to open the blinds but knew better. She couldn't take the chance a passerby could see her. She felt closed in, like the killer was getting closer.

How safe was she? Should she take down her Internet and her Facebook page? She'd loved social media and had taken advantage of it. She had displayed her photography on Pinterest and made a number of sales through it. She'd already dropped that, her old Facebook and all the art galleries she was in. She'd started a new Facebook page under her new name but she'd already deleted it. She bought a throwaway cellphone and refused to give anyone her address. She had never used the phone but she had it in case she needed to call 9-1-1.

* * *

The money would soon run out if she didn't find a good way to sell her work. She wanted to try the market days in Port Isabel and Harlingen but there was no way on earth she could sit out there in the open. She considered starting over on the Internet with a new name but she didn't know if the killer was tech-savvy. It would be her luck that he was a tech-genius. She'd read that people in the know could find anybody online.

She'd even visited the cemetery in Port Isabel one evening. She could take a name from a tombstone and become that person. She'd watched TV shows about that too but she didn't know how to get the documents she would need. How would she find out if that person had family that cared about them? It was a lot easier on TV. The truth was that she didn't know how to be a criminal.

* * *

Lester's nerves brought on a rare killer headache. He hated feeling sick when he had to constantly watch for problems in his organization. He had a crew of four drivers. Robbie and Carlos needed money to bring their families to America. Hank had been with him the shortest time but he had the most on him. When he'd threatened to tell Hank's wife about sweet little Maria, he'd found another willing driver. He'd put him with Juan because Juan had been with him the longest.

Lester knew that a family man like Juan could be manipulated. He'd learned Jorge and Rosita's names, their school and the playground they loved. He'd hired a detective buddy to follow his wife, Lourdes, and learned she went to daily Mass and then loved to stop for coffee before window shopping. She seldom bought anything but she spent plenty of time looking. He found the one thing he could use against her and his threat impacted the children. Juan would do anything for them and Lester took advantage of it.

He remembered the day Juan had caved in. "I can't do it," Juan had said.

"If you don't, your family falls apart tomorrow. No more time. Make up your mind now." Lester's voice assumed the flatness of his expression. The time for conversation had ended.

"I just can't treat people like animals," Juan headed to his pickup.

Lester raised his arm to grab him but thought better of it. He was through with games. Tomorrow the truth would come out and Juan would be destroyed. He turned away.

A cold wind chilled Juan's bones on the hot summer day. He realized Lester was most dangerous when he didn't fight back. He meant what he said and Juan's world would be crushed. He couldn't let that happen.

"What do I have to do?" Juan's voice was little more than a whisper. After a secret smile, Lester turned around.

* * *

"Just drive a truck whenever I need you."

Two years had passed and Lester still sensed the fear in Juan.

However, Lester felt his crew presented fewer issues than his boss. Fred never listened and that was dangerous. He also refused to raise Lester's share even though he took all the chances. Fred's

41

vanity was his weakness and Lester knew without a doubt that Fred thought he would be safe if they were ever caught.

* * *

Betty dragged herself through the days but nights brought the tears and anguish. She wondered if anyone had ever been so alone. Did people realize her worthlessness? The last few nights she'd realized she was no longer a productive member of society. She'd lived her life with the philosophy that everyone should do her share to make the world a better place. What had it gotten her? No one to love and no one to care. She no longer did her share but, even worse, she didn't care anymore.

If I had family, they'd be ashamed of me. There's no reason to live. Her brain ran this message through her head all night long. She thought suicide was wrong but her current life was worse.

"I need the coward's way out," she mumbled to the darkness.

* * *

"Elena is worried about a couple of people she's met and I think it's rubbing off on me tonight. But I don't know what I can do to help," Hap Lynch told his wife, Peg, as they sat on the porch watching the evening light play across the palm trees and the resaca.

"Any one I know?" Peg watched the rings the mullet made in the water when it jumped. They'd gone out to Señor Donkey's for a margarita and it felt luxurious to relax in their own private space.

"Betty, for one. She seems so depressed. Elena met her on the beach the other day. I saw her in the bookstore and she avoided everyone."

"Do you think she still hasn't recovered from her brother being in prison?"

"I think that's part of it but there's more. I don't have any real reason but she's not acting like herself. She used to enjoy talking with people."

"At least she's out and about," Peg said. "That's a good sign. After all, she found out she had a brother and he turned out to be a jerk and a murderer. I can't imagine how I'd feel."

"You're probably right. She just didn't seem her normal self."

"Who's the other one?"

"Other one what?"

"Hap, you said a 'couple of people.' Betty's one, so who's the other?"

"Yeah," Hap laughed away his embarrassment at losing his train of thought. "Michaela Flanagan— she calls herself Mick. She's scared to death. I've never seen anyone walking around in such fear. She's so closed-mouth about it that no one can help her. I think she must have faced something horrible and is running away."

43

"Another lost soul to fix, huh?" Peg smiled at this man who worried about others. "Maybe we should invite her out to dinner or drinks? What do you think? Maybe Michaela and Betty too."

"Yeah, sounds good." Hap knew Peg would care. Dinner or drinks wouldn't solve any problems but it might start a conversation. He'd contact them both tomorrow. He'd ask Elena too.

7

You have power over your mind—not outside events. Realize this and you will find strength.

Marcus Aurelius, Meditations

MATT SPOKE TO Mick last night. She'd checked the locks for the hundredth time and huddled down in her chair. She'd turned on every light in the house. It might attract attention but nothing would come out of the dark. There'd been nights when she sat in the dark so no one could see that she was home. Then she faced the darkness. It didn't matter. She'd never be safe again.

* * *

"Mick," she'd instantly recognized his voice. Tears blurred her eyes. "Mick."

"I'm here, Matt. Are you real or am I dreaming?" She looked around but he wasn't anywhere in the room.

"I'm real for this moment. I need you, sis."

"I need you too. What do you want? Where are you?" Was someone playing tricks on her? She huddled deeper in her chair.

"You think I was murdered, don't you? That's why you're so afraid. Forget about it, Mick. You need to start living your life."

"Are you saying you weren't murdered? Where are you? I can't see you."

"No, you can't see me. I'm telling you to take care of yourself. Start living your life again. Mine is over. There are things you don't know and that was for your own good. Are you taking and selling pictures?"

"Yes . . . no, I'm not. I can't, Matt. I think you were murdered and whoever it was saw me too. You ignored my question. Were you murdered?"

"Anything that happened to me, I deserved. You don't know anything so you are safe. Please, Mick. I can't face eternity if you're not all right."

"That's the problem with twins, isn't it? I depended on you. I loved you . . . no, I still love you. I can't rest until I know what happened. I don't know why I'm afraid. I shouldn't mind dying if I can see you again."

"Don't be ridiculous. Live your life. Live for both of us."

"Oh, you sound like the big brother you think you are. Remember it's only by ten minutes." Mick laughed for the first time in months."

"Mick, remember what I said. I have to go."

"You haven't answered my question." Silence was her only answer.

Matt was gone. Did she dream him or was he really here? It had to be him because he refused to answer her. If it had been a dream, she'd know the answer. Damn him, anyway. What did he mean, he deserved it. He didn't deserve to die. Matt would never do anything wrong. Well, not anything big.

Mick spent the rest of the night alternating between laughter and tears. It was so wonderful to hear his voice. She loved that bossy tone when he thought he was right. Oh God, she missed him. Why tell God? He let him die.

* * *

Peg had chosen The Chef House for a casual lunch overlooking the Gulf. She settled on the corner table closest to the window, thinking that Michaela could have her back against the wall and still enjoy the view. Hap chose the seat with his back to the view so both Michaela and Betty would see him when they looked out.

Betty gave them a tentative smile when she arrived right on time. Peg noticed she wore neither makeup nor jewelry. That was a bad sign. Betty had always enjoyed costume jewelry—usually with a dolphin or some other kind of critter.

Peg worked to keep a casual conversation flowing. She wanted to give Hap a piece of her mind for not helping. How in the world could he arrange a lunch and then clam up?

She suggested they order margaritas while they waited for Michaela.

"I shouldn't have one," Betty stared at her hands in her lap.

"How about a Coke or iced tea, then?" Peg kept her voice casual.

When Betty didn't answer, Peg changed the subject. "I invited Elena and Gloria to join us today. Elena and her dad went to Mexico and Gloria already had plans. Betty, do you and Gloria get together often?"

"No."

"Hopefully you can give her a call soon. Do you still go to Mexico often?"

"No."

"Hap," Peg turned to him.

"Sorry, I was wondering if I should give Michaela a call." Hap's sheepish smile told Peg that he realized he'd been no help.

"Betty," he said, "do you intend to go back to the museum? I stopped by the other day and they really need you to come back."

"No . I don't think so," Betty looked out over the dune.

"I guess it's been busy. Lots of visitors stop by to see if the Golden Booby has been found." One-sided conversation wasn't Hap's strong point. "Me, I'm interested in the photos of the real Brown Booby that Scarlet Colley took. She's donated them to the museum. One framed photo is at least 2'x3.' It's a beautiful shot. I'd love to see the actual bird. "Have you seen the photos?" he asked Betty.

"No. I haven't been back since . . . you know ."

"I understand but I think those photographs are worth seeing."

When Betty didn't answer, Hap continued, "We'd be happy to go with you if it would help."

"Yes, we would. I agree with Hap that you should see the photos," Peg smiled at Betty.

"I'm sure they're beautiful and I've never seen a Brown Booby, but . . . I don't know if I can."

"Well, just think about it," Hap encouraged as he caught sight of Michaela. "Here she is now."

He stood as Michaela reached the table. "We're happy you joined us. Have you been here before?"

"No," Mick took the remaining chair, thankful that she had her back to the wall. They probably planned that for me, she thought. Tears threatened as she realized how long it had been since anyone cared. Matt had always cared.

"Isn't the view wonderful?" Peg noticed Michaela's distress.

"Yes, I wish I'd brought my camera." Mick admonished herself for the lie. She hadn't touched her camera since that awful day.

Hap introduced Peg and asked, "Have you met Betty yet?"

"Not formally," Mick tried to hide her embarrassment. This was the lady who had knocked on her car window at the bookstore. Had she been rude? She couldn't remember.

"Betty is a friend and a font of information about the area. Betty, Michaela is an artist who recently moved to the island."

"Yes, I remember her," Betty's murmur could hardly be heard.

"You work at the museum, don't you?" Mick made the connection she'd failed to make at the bookstore.

"Not any more."

In the silence that ensued, Hap questioned his sanity for wanting to help two unwilling women.

The waitress came to take their orders, giving them a break from the need to fill empty space. Hap decided a conversation about food should be non-threatening to both women. He asked Peg her favorite item on the menu and she took it from there. Betty admitted that her favorite dish was migas (scrambled eggs mixed with corn tortilla, onions, chile peppers, tomatoes and cheese). "I love it with some good salsa to spice it up," she said.

"Michaela," Peg began.

"Please call me Mick."

"Mick, tell us about your artwork. What is your special interest?"

"I love nature. I am first and foremost a photographer. I may paint from some of my photographs but sometimes, they are too stunning for me to even hope to recreate."

"Have you photographed our beautiful little island?" Hap asked.

"No . . . at least not as much. I . . . I've stopped working," Mick's nervousness increased.

"May I ask why?" Hap pushed.

"Yes . . . no . . . I mean I just can't work right now." *Live your life*, Matt had said. Mick could almost hear him repeating it. *Live for both of us.*

"Are you okay?" Betty asked, concerned.

Before Mick could answer, their food arrived. Peg and Hap kept up a running conversation during dinner. Although neither Betty nor Mick had much to add, they both relaxed and enjoyed the meal.

Mick sensed Betty's despair. She understood it. Maybe she could help. Who was she kidding? She couldn't take care of herself right now. *Live your life.*

"Betty, maybe you can show me some good places to photograph sometime." Mick mentally kicked herself for offering. Betty was hesitating. Maybe she would refuse.

"Maybe." What if Mick realized she really didn't know much about the area? Would Mick reject her if she didn't find any good locations? Betty knew she'd find the island and the wildlife refuge beautiful. She could show her favorite spots along Highway 48 and around the university campus in Brownsville. "Yes, I'd like that," she smiled.

* * *

"Well, what do you think, Hap?" Peg asked as she turned onto Padre Blvd.

"It was worth all that talking," Hap admitted.

"If Elena and Gloria had been here, they would have kept the conversation alive. It would have been much easier."

* * *

Fred stayed late at the bank. He told his wife he had an appointment. He did—with his safe deposit boxes. He was finding it addictive to look at the money and know it was his. The last time he'd checked it during banking hours, one of the tellers walked into the vault. He wouldn't allow that to happen again.

He prided himself on managing his money with no one suspecting anything. He told his wife that he was contributing to his 401k and managing their investments. They lived the lifestyle she expected. They owned a nice home, both drove new cars and were paying their daughter's college tuition. His son loved golf and the whole family enjoyed their country club membership. Sure, he told them they needed to budget their money because he was saving for retirement.

* * *

The truth was that one more year of his other business would prepare him for a retirement that bank officers can only dream about. He fingered the large bills, daydreaming of a life far away from the mundane world of opening bank accounts, managing tellers and overseeing the loan department.

Tonight he replaced another stack of bills. He preferred to keep moving his money in and out of the daily flow. It felt safer even though he knew the money had been laundered so many times that it was squeaky clean. A banker could never be too careful and he placed too much value on his standing in the community to ever risk discovery.

He set up accounts in Grand Cayman that held most of his money but he needed operating capital here. Hell, he thought, what he really needed was this—the physical assurance that he had it. When he opened up the boxes, he could forget the desperation on the faces of the illegals. He knew how slim their chances were, but it wasn't his problem. I'm actually helping them, he told himself. They'd get here with or without me. I just make it easier.

Just one more year of putting up with a loser like Lester, who probably drank and partied away every dollar. No amount of money could ever bring him out of the gutter.

Fred closed the boxes, put them away and locked the vault behind him. He planned to stop and buy flowers on the way home. His wife trusted him and he appreciated that.

8

Friendship is the only cement that will ever hold the world together.

Woodrow T. Wilson

"I'VE INVITED A friend along," Betty said as Mick opened the passenger door and saw the stranger in the back seat. "This is Gloria."

"Hi, Mick. It's so nice to meet you," Gloria's smile spread across her face.

"Hello." Mick loved the sincerity of her smile.

"Betty tells me you're an artist. I love painting. We have art leagues on the island and in Port Isabel. On Fridays, a group of us get together to paint. You should join us." Gloria's enthusiasm made Mick itch for her camera.

Did she really miss it that much? Remembering the conversation, she asked, "What do you paint and in what medium?"

"Whatever suits me at the moment. I use watercolors, acrylic and oils. I'm working on a children's book and I sell my cards at my son's shop."

"I bet your paintings are as sunny as you," Mick said.

I made a smart move, Betty told herself as the two talked. I can fade into the background while Gloria keeps Mick entertained. She knew Hap and Peg should be pleased with her for following up with Mick, and Gloria would make the outing comfortable. She really had nothing to add to the conversation anyway. Two artistic women would have little interest in her.

Betty parked the car at the convention center. "I wanted to show you the boardwalk first," she told Mick. She hung back as they meandered along the sidewalk. At the boardwalk, she lagged even more, staying close enough to hear their conversation. Soon the voices drifted into murmurings as Betty focused on a Roseate Spoonbill and two Snowy Egrets. Their grace and beauty threatened the numbness that enveloped her heart.

"Betty doesn't realize her natural appreciation of beauty houses a creative soul," Gloria whispered to Mick.

Betty's reaction eclipsed her shyness and depression. For a moment she forgot her pain. Then reality hit her. How could a God that created such wondrous creatures also create someone like DL Casa? That was the question she couldn't get past. She only had to look around to find beauty—in nature and the people she knew here in the Valley. Her world had known sunshine and purpose until a new-found brother crushed her into nothingness.

Could Mick and Gloria see the darkness that blanketed her soul? She and DL shared some of the same DNA. She had suffered from his black heart. Would she become like him?

"Betty, do you paint?" Mick intruded on Betty's thoughts.

"No."

"I've asked her to come to our Friday sessions," Gloria said. "You should see some of the beautiful pieces she knits. She has a flair for colors."

Betty's blush was her only answer. She hadn't held her knitting needles since Carol's murder.

"I introduced her to Mary Russell Muchmore," Gloria said. "You've become friends, haven't you, Betty?"

"Yes, but I haven't talked to her in a while."

Mick's curiosity was aroused. "Who's Mary Russell Muchmore?"

"A winter Texan who takes to people like a duck to water. She loves our Valley and is active in her church and charities while she's here. Plus she loves to knit. I will have to introduce you to her."

Betty barely listened as her thoughts turned to Mary Russell. She'd been a friend when she needed one. Mary Russell had been a part of her life before the murder. Betty had lost contact with most of her old friends. She couldn't face them knowing her brother was a murderer. It had taken all her strength to invite Gloria today.

She realized her life centered around one horrible event over which she'd had no control. She would gladly have taken Carol's place.

"I think we're ready to go," Gloria interrupted Betty's thoughts. "How about Sea Turtle Inc next?"

By the time they left the turtles Betty realized she was enjoying the day, as well as Mick and Gloria. She couldn't believe she'd actually forgotten DL while she watched the turtles.

* * *

The day brought hope to Mick. She could easily fall in love with the area and the people if she were free. She marveled that she actually walked the boardwalk without the fear that haunted her. She hadn't forgotten Matthew. In fact, several times she'd wished he were there with her. No, she could never forget him, but for a few moments she'd forgotten her fear of his killers. She'd done what Matthew wanted—she'd lived her life for a little while.

However, in the dark of night, she knew that forgetting was foolish—a way to get caught off guard. Somewhere, someone wanted her dead. She felt it in her bones.

* * *

Gloria turned on the ballgame and set up her paint equipment. Tonight she'd paint a beautiful young woman walking the boardwalk. She'd include the Roseate Spoonbill and the Snowy Egrets. When she finished, she would give it to Mick.

She smiled as she picked up her brush.

* * *

Lourdes cried as Juan held her in his arms. He loved holding her at night but always dreaded the tears.

"Baby, what's wrong?" he stroked her bare back.

"I'm so afraid. They are picking up more illegals everyday. Josie, the mother of one of Jorge's classmates, was taken to the immigration center two nights ago. The family thinks she will be deported." The tears flowed and Lourdes couldn't continue.

Juan waited patiently, dreading what he knew was coming. He felt so helpless.

"I know they're going to find me," Lourdes sobbed harder. "I can't live without my babies. What would I do?" Juan wished that just once she'd say she couldn't live without him. He wanted to ask if she would miss him but he was afraid of the answer. Better just to hold her and know I love her, he thought.

"Lourdes . . . Baby, they won't find you and if they do, we'll get a good lawyer. He'll prove how much Rosita and Jorge need you. I need you, too."

"We couldn't afford a lawyer. They'd send me back. I've been here so long, I hardly remember my home in Mexico. I have no one there since the Cartel killed my father."

"Don't worry. I'm saving money and maybe there'll never discover you anyway. Your English is as good or better than most people born here."

"You're a good provider, Juan, a good man. You take care of us." Her tears slowed and he felt her relax.

"Go to sleep. I'm here and I love you," he whispered softly. She hadn't said what he wanted to hear but he was proud that she considered him a good provider. *Please God, don't let her ever find out that I'm not a good man.*

As Lourdes drifted off to sleep, Juan saw the faces of the last load of illegals he delivered. He saw no hope for them. He brushed a lock of hair from Lourdes' face and felt her pain.

* * *

Lester drank the last of his Corona and signaled the waiter for another. Nothing lessened his anger with Fred. The idiot didn't have a clue about the real world. He thought about the conversation they'd had earlier.

"Lester, you worry about unimportant things. I've told you a thousand times to forget about Matthew." Fred tried to turn the conversation. "Think about the thousands of fools still willing to pay us good money to get across the border."

"I know but it'll do us no good if we end up in prison."

"We won't. You've built an organization that works and not a one of them will ever give us up. You were right to pick people who had a lot to lose." Fred was always counting the next dollar.

"You're right. Our delivery teams are okay but Michaela could be a loose cannon. We need her out of the way and that's easy enough to do if we can find her. She can't be selling her work anymore or she'd be on the Internet. It's like she just disappeared."

"That's good for us. Let her be gone, Lester. Get your mind on building a bigger team. We could double our runs and pocket a lot of money."

"That's part of the problem, Fred. You only think about the money and you pocket most of it. I get a lousy twenty percent and I do all the work."

"You're a fool. You only have to worry about the deliveries and then you walk away. Who do you think makes the connections and sets up the loads? Who has set up the logistics for the whole operation? You do one small part and I pay you generously to do it. If you don't like it, get out!"

Lester's hand moved toward his pocket but Fred's hand was quicker. "Don't even think about it!" Fred tightened his grip on Lester's arm.

"Damn you!" Lester stopped resisting—for now. Let Fred think he'd won this round. He needed to get back to his search for Michaela.

"Another one?" the bartender asked.

"No, I have work to do." Lester slapped a $20 bill down on the bar and headed home to his computer.

9

If you haven't any charity in your heart, you have the worst kind of heart trouble.

Bob Hope

ROBERTO RODRIGUEZ-GARCIA ARRIVED on time for his leisurely breakfast with Maria. She was a good sister but she was a morning person. Roberto had long ago given up early mornings. However, he had to make it to Manuel's before 10 a.m. to get the breakfast special.

"Bert, I'm so happy you're here. We have to catch up before I head back to San Antonio. I've barely seen you so I think you have a new girlfriend."

"You've always been a nosy one," he laughed as he gave her a bear hug. "Maybe I want to hear about your love life. I'm sure it's more exciting than mine."

"No. Johnny and I are fine. We're still hoping to start a family."

"That means you're definitely having fun."

Oh, you," she slapped at his shoulder. "You never change."

"I hope not, *hermanita*."

"Seriously, Bert. Are you dating anyone special since you lost Carol? I do wish I'd met her."

"I wish so, too. She was a special lady but it was all a horrible affair. I keep trying to forget it but I haven't forgotten Carol. But back to you. Are you really happy?"

"Yes, don't worry about me. Johnny's not as much of a playboy as you!"

"Hah! I've never been a playboy. I'm just still on the search for true love. I thought it had a chance with Carol but I know she wouldn't want me to stop living."

"She must have been a special lady, Bert."

"She was. But let's forget serious stuff and enjoy some good food."

As if on cue, Frank appeared with two cups of coffee. "Good to see you, Bert."

"Who's the beautiful lady?" Jay rushed up to the table.

"Ah, you two. Frank serves me coffee and Jay tries to steal my date," Roberto winked at Maria.

"You two don't stand a chance with my handsome Bert around," she played along.

"Jay looks so sad we better tell the truth," Bert said. "Maria is my baby sister."

"Does that mean she's available?" Jay grinned.

"Nope, she's married—to a big strong man who loves to chase off other suitors. Now take my order, you clowns."

Jay and Frank laughed and settled down to the business at hand.

After they ordered, Maria said, "I had the strangest beach encounter the other day. I saw an older woman picking up shells. I asked if she had found anything exciting, and you would have thought I was from Mars. Plus she looked like she'd been crying."

"Probably someone having a bad day and you startled her. I think the beach brings out emotional responses in some people," Roberto theorized.

"But there's more. When I told her you were my brother, she nearly passed out. I didn't know even your name has such a strong—or strange—effect on women." Maria loved to tease Bert.

"Did you get her name?"

"She ran, Bert. She actually ran away. I don't think you're having much luck with the ladies down here. Guess your reputation preceded you."

"You're enjoying this way too much, little one. I'll get even."

As they left the restaurant, Maria asked, "Want to watch the sunset tonight?"

"Sure, what do you have in mind?"

"You really do? I was kidding 'cause I figured you had a date."

"Well, little one, that would be preferable but since I don't, I'm available. How about a late dinner at Louie's?"

"Awesome." Maria reached up and planted a kiss on his cheek.

After they went their separate ways, Roberto's thoughts returned to Maria's story. *Who could she be? I can't imagine anyone being afraid of me. I've never intentionally offended a woman, especially not an older woman. But then, Maria's young. Anyone over forty is probably old to her.*

* * *

Gloria woke up late with Betty on her mind. It only took a few minutes yesterday to figure out her game. Betty had invited her to carry the conversation with Mick. Gloria wasn't about to play that game. Betty needed to get back out in the world and move past that awful experience with her brother. Her shame was understandable but nothing had been her fault. There's only one way to help, Gloria told herself.

Betty answered on the third ring. She would have ignored it from anyone else but Gloria had done her a favor yesterday.

"Hi, Betty," Gloria began. "I had a wonderful time yesterday. It was great to see you and I enjoyed Mick too."

"Thank you for coming. I don't think Mick would have enjoyed it if you hadn't been there. She's tough to talk to."

"Like I told you, I did it because I told Hap Lynch I would."

"Not a problem but now I want a return favor."

"What is that?" Betty tensed.

"Not much. Just company for dinner tonight. Would you join me—or rather us—at Louie's tonight?"

"Who's 'us'?"

"Mick and me. I figured we warmed her up a little yesterday. We might as well go a step further today. I think Louie's will be fun and we can hang around for the sunset. It's supposed to be a beautiful evening."

"Well, I don't know . . ."

"Come on, Betty. Mick needs our help. She's really quite lovely if she isn't worried about her problems. Mick asked if you were coming." *A little white lie was okay if it was for a good cause, wasn't it?*

"Oh, well . . ."

"Come on. Why don't I pick you up at 7:00? It'll be fun and maybe I can talk you into attending one of my painting classes."

"I'll go tonight but I don't have any artistic talent."

"Great. See you tonight." Gloria gave herself a thumbs up.

* * *

Juan's stomach growled when he walked through the door and caught a whiff of Lourde's Carne Guisada. He counted his wife's cooking as one of life's blessings. His two greatest blessings ran to greet him.

"Papá, I missed you. I helped Mama bake a cake today.

You get to taste it," Rosita chattered.

"I will be happy to be your taste tester," he laughed.

"Do you know what tomorrow is?"

"Let me see. Is it your dentist appointment?"

"No, Papá, it's my birthday. Don't you remember?"

"Of course I do. That means we'll have cake again tomorrow."

"But I won't have to bake it," Rosita looked at her mama.

"Quit talking, Rosita. It's my turn," Jorge stomped his foot. "Papá, I got an 'A' on my math test today."

"*Bien*, son, I'm proud of you. You keep studying so you don't have to work so hard when you grow up," Juan beamed with pride. His son already showed a determination to do well in school. Hopefully he would make an honest living and would never know what his papá did.

"Papá, am I smart?" Rosita asked.

"Yes, you are, little one. You'll do well in school but now we celebrate Jorge's achievement."

"And tomorrow we celebrate my birthday."

"Dinner time," Lourdes hugged her children. "I hope you both grow up to be as smart as your papá."

Shame slammed through Juan, spoiling his appetite and his mood. He wanted out of smuggling but Lester held the key to his family's happiness. *Please God, help me find a way.*

* * *

Gloria felt like a mother hen as Michaela and Betty warmed to conversation. She had worried that she was pushing too hard but both seemed to have a good time. The sky over the bay seemed to anticipate the sunset with tinges of orange. The artist in her succumbed to nature's display and the conversation faded from her consciousness.

"Gloria," a male voice brought her back to her surroundings.

She turned around to see Roberto Rodriguez-Garcia smiling as he walked toward her. He held the hand of a pretty young woman.

"Bert, how nice to see you." She didn't notice the change in Betty. "Is this your little sister? She even looks like you."

"*Gracias, mi querida*," Bert took Gloria's hand to his lips. Maria snapped a couple of photos with her iPhone. Bert turned to Betty. "And here is my lovely friend, Miss Betty."

She wanted to melt into the woodwork. Memories flashed as fresh as the day they were made. She hadn't seen Roberto since DL's trial and she would have done anything to avoid this meeting. If only she'd stayed home. All her timidity and apprehension erased the comfort she had felt with Michaela and Gloria. *Please God, don't let him mention Carol or DL.*

Betty's tension enveloped the group and for a moment conversation ceased. Gloria and Maria salvaged the awkward meeting with a stream of chatter about the sunset, the food and anything else they could think of. Soon Betty, Roberto and Michaela relaxed. With pleasantries exchanged, Roberto and Maria left to find a table. Fireworks lit up the nighttime sky and they focused on the display.

Neither Betty nor Mick said a word the entire time. Mick kept her questions to herself but wondered what about Roberto threw Betty into a panic. If she remembered correctly from the newspapers and trial, Roberto had been dating Carol Flores at the time of the murder. Surely that wasn't enough for Betty's response.

By the time they left Louie's, Gloria felt like she'd worked for hours. When Betty got out of Gloria's car, she ran to her door. Inside she turned the deadlock, switched on every light in the house, drew all the blinds and sat down in her favorite chair. She wished she had a cat. When her Elsie was alive, she'd curl up on her lap and comfort her. But she had to face the night alone. She'd tried, God knows, how hard it had been but she had made the effort. She knew she'd made everyone uncomfortable but Roberto had paralyzed her. Memories pounded in her head. She took two Tylenol and prowled. Carol had tried to hide her joy each time Roberto walked in the museum. She hadn't seen it at the time but it all made sense later. Roberto's gallantry, the police suspecting him, DL making a fool of her, the newspaper article that quoted him calling her "wimpy and boring," Roberto testifying at the trial.

Michaela couldn't wait to get home and dig through some old photographs of Matthew. If he'd been here tonight, he'd have known what to say and do. But then if he were here, she'd still be at home. She wouldn't be more than a thousand miles away trying to bring her brother back through photographs.

Gloria sighed after she dropped Betty off. It had started so well and ended back at square one. Oh well, there were always new opportunities. At home, she painted tonight's sunset and planned her next line of attack.

* * *

"Bert, that's the lady I saw at the beach, the one I told you about," Maria took her seat. "How do you know her?"

"Chiquita, she was Carol's assistant at the museum. She was always quite shy but now, I think she's hurting inside. Her half-brother is the one who killed my Carol."

"I'm so sorry. That's why she reacted so strangely to your name. I think she needs kindness."

"You have a loving heart, Maria. I agree but I don't know how to help her."

Bert's thoughts had turned to Michaela. He never had the chance to greet her but he felt she needed his help. The sadness written on her beautiful face drew him in.

Before she went to sleep, Maria checked her Facebook and posted several of the photos she'd taken all day.

* * *

Lester spent most of the night on his computer. He'd given up on finding Michaela through her artwork. He hadn't found one reference to any recent works or appearances. He'd even looked up international shows but never found her name listed. If she'd given up photography, he had no idea how far she'd run but she had to surface somewhere. He'd called in a favor and found out she hadn't used any of her old credit cards. He suspected she may be using a different name. He would find her. It was only a matter of time.

* * *

Fred watched a movie with his wife until she fell asleep. He tiptoed to his study, turned on his computer and checked the stock market. Even his legitimate money in the US was performing well. He had arranged two more pick ups this week and both would be full loads. The money gods were smiling on him. He smiled back.

10

Try to be a rainbow in someone's cloud.

Maya Angelou, Letter to My Daughter

HAP LYNCH LET the phone ring until it went to Betty's voicemail. "Betty, please give me a call. I have a favor to ask of you." Elena had called last night and given him an idea. She had gone home to Jefferson City.

"Do you think it will work, Hap?" Doubt tinged Peg's voice.

"She needs prodding and there's no one better than Luke to demand a reaction."

"For sure. He'll demand some petting time and that will be good for Betty."

"As long as she doesn't see through my ploy," Hap answered. "I should call Gloria and see if she's getting Betty out of the house." Hap took Luke for a walk and forgot about calling.

When Betty hadn't returned his call by evening, he again thought about calling Gloria. His thoughts turned to Mick. Helping frightened women was harder work than any investigation. He was sure Gloria was the answer but then he wondered if this job was too much even for her. He wished Elena were here to help. Her youthful enthusiasm was contagious to even the most weary adult.

He checked his Facebook before bedtime and was surprised to see a message from Roberto Rodriquez- Garcia. He hadn't thought of him since the investigation. Now he wanted to have coffee. Curious, he agreed to meet him the next morning at Grapevine.

When Hap arrived, he found Roberto in a back booth. After they ordered coffee, Roberto leaned into the booth. "I need some information and I thought of you."

"What is it?" Hap stirred his steaming coffee.

"You remember Michaela Flanagan? I ran into her last night and I think she needs our help."

"What makes you think that?"

"I've never seen such sadness and fear before. I didn't get a chance to talk to her but she tugged at my heart."

"What do you think we can do?" Hap wondered what lay behind Roberto's concern.

"I don't know. That's why I contacted you. Do you think she's afraid of someone? Do you have any idea why? I don't often get these feelings, but I'm worried about her."

"Roberto—"

"Call me Bert, please."

"Bert, I don't know what we can do. I've seen the same anxiety in her but she's extremely protective of her privacy. I don't think she'd talk about it to any of us." Hap didn't want his wariness to show. He didn't know Bert that well, but he had no reason to doubt him.

"I think you're right but there must be something we can do. Could we watch over her? I mean, I know this isn't a matter for the police but maybe you and I could keep an eye on her."

"There can be a fine line between watching over and stalking. She hasn't asked either of us for help. Until she does, we don't have any right to watch her."

"Hap, please trust me on this. I don't mean her harm. I'm truly worried about her. I feel it in my heart."

"Is that all you feel in your heart?"

"Yes, of course. I really don't know her. Forget it. I guess I'm over-reacting. I'm sorry I bothered you."

"Bert, you didn't bother me. I don't know whether or not you're over-reacting. I think she's deathly afraid of something and I've tried to draw her out but nothing works. I had suggested Betty get back together with one of her old friends. She's got the sort of personality that draws people and if Michaela responds to anyone, it will probably be her."

"Could that friend be Gloria?"

"Yes, how did you know?"

"I ran into them last night at Louie's. Gloria, Michaela and Betty. You remember Betty, don't you? Carol's assistant?"

"Yes, I know Betty. I'm glad to hear they were out together. So what happened?"

"Nothing. Betty almost went into shock when she saw me. I have no idea why. She was always friendly to me before."

"Bert, maybe she hasn't gotten over Carol's murder and in her mind, you're probably connected to Carol and the horrible scene. I doubt it's anything personal."

"I know but it was a shock. I would never have approached her if I'd known. After we left, my sister, Maria, told me she ran into Betty on the beach and my name had the same reaction. She has nothing to fear from me. I can't imagine what she went through when she realized her own half-brother used her to get into the museum."

"Look, I've been concerned too. I'm trying to help both Betty and Michaela. My wife feels the same concern you feel. If I make any progress, I'll let you know. In the meantime, be very careful if you're trying to watch out for her. You have nothing to go on and you don't want to get in trouble with the police. Okay?"

"Okay, as long as you are doing something. You will let me know, won't you?"

"Yes. I appreciate your concern for both of them. You've moved up a notch in my book." Hap smiled.

* * *

Lester scanned through the list he'd downloaded. He'd twisted arms to get the information but it was worth it. She hadn't changed her Arizona driver's license so maybe she hadn't left the state.

Michaela Riley was scared and that gave him the advantage. How he wished he'd taken care of her at the same time as Matthew. Now he had a loose end to tie up. If she'd changed her name, as he was beginning to suspect, it would be harder to find her. He picked up his cell phone and placed a call to the man who'd caused her to run. Maybe he could help find her. A hired gun had to know how to find people. Lester agreed to pay the man's price when he found her. Any more action would be negotiated at that time.

He didn't have time for this. Fred was stepping up the number of loads. Lester didn't know how long it would last but he was living the good life now. Only Michaela's whereabouts worried him.

* * *

Juan wondered if he was the only one to notice Lester's distraction. Something was bothering him. If he could find out what it was, it might give him a way to escape from Lester's hold. His nightly prayer was to end the smuggling—both for the poor victims and for his family. Maybe God heard his prayer.

* * *

Gloria didn't believe in giving up and she bought into the old adage, "If you fall off a horse, get back on again." She planned to invite Betty and Michaela to lunch in Port Isabel. She might even call Bert and make sure he didn't show up at the same place. She felt Betty needed her the most after last night. Bert had really thrown her for a loop and that showed how deeply she still suffered. She simply couldn't be ignored. Gloria thought she wouldn't answer her phone so she'd stop by her house. If she got it organized today, they could have lunch tomorrow. This time she'd make sure it worked out better.

Michaela gave a hesitant yes after Gloria begged her to help her with Betty. *She really has a good heart,* Gloria thought. *Hopefully by helping Betty, we'll help her.*

Betty was sorry she answered the door because Gloria wouldn't take no for an answer. She finally agreed when Gloria asked for her help with Michaela.

After reporting her progress to Hap and calling Bert, Gloria spent the day relaxing. The next day she picked up Betty and they met Michaela at Pelican Station at noon. Gloria requested a corner table on the upper level where they had more privacy and could still enjoy the bay. By the time their food arrived, she had achieved a level of comfortable conversation. After lunch she suggested they visit the Laguna Madre Art Gallery. Betty and Mick lost track of time as they wandered through the gallery. Betty went next door to Tesori's to visit June and check out her latest jewelry collections.

After the gallery, Gloria suggested a walk around Lighthouse Square. Michaela begged off but Betty appreciated the opportunity to walk around. All in all, Gloria counted the day a success and knew that both Betty and Michaela had enjoyed it. She felt sure they both were emerging from whatever darkness had smothered them.

* * *

Happy for the first time since Carol's murder, Betty checked her messages. Nothing but yesterday's call from Hap Lynch. She returned his call. Hap had difficulty hiding his astonishment when she readily agreed to babysitting Luke. They made arrangements for the next day.

Michaela felt so comfortable she stopped by the Blue Marlin to pick up some cereal and milk. Although she was cautious, she didn't let fear overpower her. She decided to browse through the produce section but froze when someone called her name. Afraid to move but wanting to run for cover, she did nothing. Even when she saw it was only Roberto, she couldn't move.

In his surprise at seeing her, Roberto had called out before he thought. He wanted to kick himself for causing her distress. No, it was more than distress. He had thrown her into a panic. Charm and casual conversations seemed to be his best weapons. Gradually some of the tension drained from her mind and her body. Unable to resist his ridiculous efforts at gallantry, she hid the beginnings of a smile. Roberto saw it.

Satisfied that she had relaxed enough to smile, he knew it was time to make his exit. After apologizing for not acknowledging her at Louie's, he left with a lift in his spirits and a sense of accomplishment.

Michaela watched him walk away. She knew he probably charmed every woman he met, but it didn't matter. It had been too long since she enjoyed a chance encounter with a man.

* * *

"Matthew," she whispered in the dim light room. "Please come back again. I have so much to tell you."

She waited but met only silence.

"I am trying to live as you suggested. I need you to know that."

She propped her head up with her right arm. Sleep eluded her even as a growing sense of living filled her. She so wanted Matthew to understand the gift he had given her.

"I actually talked to a man in the grocery store today. His name is Roberto. But he prefers Bert. I remember him from DL Casa's murder trial. I had a good day with two new friends. I'm living, Matthew."

She knew that Matthew wouldn't come tonight but she prayed he heard her. She lay her head on her pillow and soon she was lost in a dreamworld of life before he left her.

11

Shared joy is a double joy; shared sorrow is half a sorrow.

Swedish Proverb

BERT COULDN'T STOP thinking about Michaela. He told himself that it was nothing more than concern but he knew better. After Carol was killed, he didn't think he'd meet another woman who'd spark his interest. Michaela was younger than him. He didn't know her age but he bet there was at least fifteen years' difference. She'd still be young when age slowed him down. But then, he wasn't planning a relationship. He worried about her. He wanted to help her overcome her fear and resolve its cause. That was all.

He needed her phone number and he didn't know how to get it. He decided Gloria probably knew it but he didn't know if she'd give it to him. She saw beneath his displays of charm and she was no fool. Maybe he'd have better luck trying Hap Lynch. In the end he'd called them both but neither felt free to give out Michaela's number. Gloria finally told him that Michaela loved nature. He'd check the boardwalk, the birding center and the other wildlife spots until he found her.

Luck had always followed him and his search for Michaela was no exception. He accidentally ran into her the next evening on the boardwalk. As they talked, she showed him the photos she'd taken. She didn't tell him it was one of the few times she'd had her hands on her camera since she came to the island. The birds she had captured turned into his friends as she relaxed more and more. To his surprise, she readily accepted his invitation for yogurt at UMix.

She drove her own car and arrived a few minutes after him. After they taste-tested several flavors, they laughed as they filled their cups and heaped on the toppings. With such a scrumptious dessert, the conversation flowed easily. By the time they parted, she had agreed to have dinner with him the next evening. She even agreed to let him pick her up at her condo. It would be difficult to know which of them was more surprised.

As Bert drove home, his thoughts returned to their age difference but it didn't really matter. He hadn't felt so alive since Carol—if he ever had. He'd cared for Carol and if she'd lived, he would have asked for her hand in marriage.

But after her death, he realized she hadn't been the soul mate of his dreams. He'd never know if they could have had a happy marriage. So many men counted happiness as sexual satisfaction and a wife who catered to their every whim. He didn't want that. He wanted a woman who had her own dreams and understood his. He wanted someone to walk beside him with confidence and pride. God knew he wasn't worthy but he could dream. Then again, maybe with Michaela it was only sexual tension.

Mick looked in her mirror. She couldn't believe the woman facing her had so readily agreed to a date. She was carrying Matthew's advice to extremes. What had happened to her caution? Yes, Bert was charming but she didn't know anything about him. She suspected he was considerably older but that didn't matter to her. Trust and respect were more important. She would have to learn if he were worthy of either. In the meantime, the glowing face in the mirror made her nervous.

By the time he picked her up the next evening, Mick felt she had herself under control again. She would keep the evening casual and put the brakes on. However, when she looked at him, she saw the same crazy glow that had greeted her in the mirror.

Afterward Mick couldn't remember any of their conversation but she'd loved every minute of it. Bert proved to be much more than charming. He loved books and classical music, and his favorite place was a bookstore. Photography appealed to him and they discussed topics such as lighting, setting and the Golden Circle.

He enjoyed traveling by car, stopping whenever something caught his attention. He especially loved architecture. Dear God, could a man be more tailor-made for her? Had God sent Bert to heal her broken heart and terrified soul? Of course, she'd said yes to a visit to the Brownsville Historical Museum the next day.

As the days flew by, she grew more trusting. When Gloria called again, Mick told her about their dates. She was relieved that Gloria approved. That strengthened her faith in her own judgment. Gloria arranged another lunch. Mick met them at Lady & the Pit. She found it hard to converse with Betty after Gloria had warned her against mentioning Bert. After all, he filled her mind.

Once again, Gloria carried the conversation. Betty related her "Luke" dog-sitting experiences. He'd entertained her with his energetic playfulness but more than that, petting him gave her comfort. She didn't tell Hap or her new friends that she had felt needed for the first time since DL entered her life. She and Mick laughed at Gloria's stories about her early years in the Valley. They shared memories of the days before South Padre Island grew into a flourishing tourist destination. They knew many of the same people—even some who had passed away. Mick felt they were all becoming friends.

Life was good with one exception. Except for his lips touching the back of her hand, Bert had never kissed her.

* * *

The man smiled when he saw the photo. He dug out the old picture he'd used before to verify it was the same woman. Even though he only had a first name, he had a location. He picked up his phone.

"I found her," he didn't believe in small talk.

It took Lester a minute to focus. "Where?" Juan and Hank had delivered another load. They'd herded the migrants into the barn and Lester had collected the money and divvied it up.

"South Padre Island."

"How did you find her?"

"Doesn't matter." He wasn't about to admit it was a simple Facebook post. An acquaintance had liked a photo from Louie's Backyard, a place he knew well. As a Mexican National, he could roam around the island without generating any attention. That was the beauty of the border region. So many of his countrymen legally crossed the border daily to work and to play. Their women crossed to shop. For years, the Texans had crossed into Mexico as easily, but now they were afraid—with good reason. He knew because he was part of the reason.

"I'll meet you there."

"I don't need you. I can take care of things."

"No, I will meet you there. Nothing happens until I get there, understand?"

"Yeah."

"I mean it, dammit. You make a move before I get there, you'll not only lose your pay, I'll make sure the authorities know who's guilty."

"Don't ever threaten me again. You won't like my payback." He cut Lester off and pocketed his phone.

Lester cursed and threw his phone across the yard.

He needed a strategy but his blood was boiling and he couldn't think clearly. A wave of dizziness made him reach for the nearest tree. He slid down along the trunk and waited for his heart to stop its erratic beating and for the sudden pain between his shoulder blades to subside. Years ago a doctor had suggested anger management classes. He had changed doctors.

His dizziness soon turned to drowsiness and as the pain went away, he napped. Juan slipped past Lester. He'd come back to ask him a question when his phone rang. Hearing one side of a conversation is tough to interpret but Juan heard enough to grasp that some woman was in danger from Lester and the person on the other end. He played the conversation in his mind again as he drove home.

Calmer when he awoke, Lester picked up his phone. He had to let Fred know he'd be away for a few days. A sick relative was always a good excuse. Never mind that he wouldn't cross the street to see any of his family.

Lester would start the long, boring 1,100-mile drive early in the morning. With Michaela dead, there would be no more threats to their cash cow.

In Mexico, the man cleaned his rifle and packed it for travel. He chose two handguns, loaded his ammo, and packed a bag. He'd built a special fishing bed with plenty of cubby holes for equipment. He carried poles, tackle and camping equipment in all the compartments. He placed his working equipment in the false bottom in the bed of the truck. He threw in a grill, chairs, a sleeping bag and a heavy box filled with surf boards and other water equipment. He carried no drugs, had no record and Border Patrol never asked him to unload the bed. He was just another Mexican National vacationing on South Padre Island.

Once he was in Texas, he drove to Harlingen to visit a woman he knew. He never drank or partied before a job but he found a night of sex relaxed him. Mindy pleased him more than most. Although he made no commitments to any woman, he told each one he cared and that he would call whenever he was in town. He visited many border towns and many women.

* * *

Behind the smile Fred gave a client, fury threatened to boil over. That damn Lester probably didn't have a relative in the world—at least not one who would speak to him. Lester was up to something and that worried him. Sometimes he felt like he had him under control and other times he realized no one can control an idiot. Lester was all temper and aggression—ready to fly apart at one wrong word. That made him dangerous. His instability threatened the whole organization. Something would have to be done in the near future. He would hold out as long as he thought he still had the upper hand. Then Lester would have to go. The business came first.

He needed Lester to keep the men in line. That was his strength. Fred suspected he motivated by fear or bribery but Lester never gave his secrets away. The one thing Fred knew for sure was that Lester had built a smooth-running organization. It would be a pity to lose him but he couldn't waste time. The entire smuggling business faced constant threats from legal or government crackdowns. If the Mexican government began to function effectively, the cartels could be threatened and the flow of illegals could dwindle. There was too much he couldn't control so he'd let nothing or no one he could control stand in his way.

12

Change is the law of life. And those who look only to the past or present are certain to miss the future.

John F. Kennedy

"WOULD YOU LIKE to go to the art show at the new convention center in Port Isabel, my lovely Michaela?" Bert already knew what her answer would be.

"I'd love it. But Bert, please call me Mick. You asked me to call you Bert and I do. I like people I care about to call me Mick and I want you to."

"I'll try but Michaela sounds of grace and beauty. You possess both, my dear."

Then hold me and kiss me, her heart begged. Surely it showed in her eyes. "Oh, how I love your gallantry," was the answer Bert heard.

He struggled to hold back his desire to touch her. He still didn't see the light of complete trust in her eyes and he didn't want to frighten her. Bert was beginning to think in forever terms. He could picture growing old with this sensitive woman, but she had to have the same vision before he let his passion rule.

"So what time will you pick me up?" Michaela broke into his thoughts.

"It's open all day but I thought maybe we'd have dinner at Pirate's Landing and then attend the evening reception."

"Would you mind going a little early so I have plenty of time to enjoy the art?"

"How about an early dinner around 5:00, and then we can get there in plenty of time before the reception? We can stay as late as you'd like."

"I'd love it and I'll be ready."

"Will you do me a favor?"

"What?"

"Would you wear the starfish necklace I gave you?"

"It's beautiful and yes, of course I will." Her smile told him much more than her words. She wanted to please him and that put a smile in his heart.

"And will you think beautiful thoughts about our little island?"

"Yes, and the time we've spent together here. I love it, Bert."

Mick wore a white sundress that showcased the gold starfish against her tanned skin. She felt beautiful tonight and she liked thinking of them as a couple. She knew she was falling in love with him but she knew so little of his past. She wondered what had happened to the women in his life before Carol? Why was this handsome, kind man available? Should she be concerned?

She had never been in his home and she never invited him into hers. It struck her how little they shared except for a few dinners and enjoyable conversations. Where was her caution when she needed it most?

"A penny for your thoughts," his gentle smile pleased her.

"I was thinking of what a wonderful evening we're going to have," she lied.

Bert knew it for what it was.

Dinner proved to be wonderful. The bay was a rare deep blue and the pelicans lazily swam or sunned themselves on the pier. Several dolphin-watch boats drifted by and the gulls trailed after them. Mick loved the skyline of the island on these clear days. She knew that the evening fog would soon soften the view to a multicolored sensory delight.

When they arrived at the art show, only a few people strolled through the displays. The caterers were putting the finishing touches on the hors d'oeuvres. Bert asked Michaela to lead the way and he followed with a watchful eye. He didn't know why he felt the need to protect this woman. She'd never shared the reason for her fear. She'd told him she had a traditional childhood, that both her parents were gone and that she had a brother who died.

As he watched her, he realized she was a different person than the frightened Michaela he had first met. She was overcoming her fear and opening herself to people. He found it a beautiful process to watch. What bothered him was not knowing what the threat had been. Was it over or was she simply pushing it away? He needed to find out but he didn't want to ask. He didn't want to push her back into that memory.

Bert saw Hap and Peg Lynch walk in. He'd try to get Hap aside for a private conversation. His nerves were on end tonight and there didn't seem to be a reason.

* * *

"Let's do it like before," Lester told him.

"We need more time to scope it out. There may be a better approach." The man realized the island offered fewer opportunities but he knew Lester wouldn't think it through.

"No, I don't have a lot of time and that worked slick before. Besides, what's good enough for Matthew is good enough for his sister. Sort of poetic justice or some such thing."

"Look at the escape routes on the island. They don't exist."

"What do you suggest?"

"Time. Poor planning causes botched jobs. I don't work in a hurry."

"You will if you want my money."

The man knew he should walk away but he was already here. This would be the last call he'd ever take from Lester.

"You said she is attending the art show at the Port Isabel convention center tonight, right?" Lester asked.

"Yes. I've only been here a few days. That's the first I've been able to verify."

"Tonight will work. You can wait in her condo. When she gets home, do it."

"Do it? God, you can't be that stupid. It would have to be a silent hit where I could walk away."

"I'll be waiting in the car. It will work. No, I'll come in and see her body. When I have proof, you get paid."

"If I even considered it, you couldn't come in. Besides, I get paid when the job is done. You take my word for it and I leave. I will be back in Mexico before the body is discovered. That has to be the plan. Take it or leave it."

"You do it tonight and I'll have the car waiting. We'll be off the island in plenty of time for you to get back to Mexico."

The loathing on the man's face made Lester cringe, but he thought he could trust the man to tell him the truth because he would want more work in the future. But he didn't trust anyone enough to put out money before he had proof a job was done. Truth is, he learned long ago to trust no one. His old man had taught him that. He'd taught him to steal and then disappeared when he got caught. The police found a garage of stolen goods where, as far as they knew, Lester lived alone. With no alibis and no proof his dad had ever been there, he went to prison while his dad went free. Only a fool puts trust in another man and Lester didn't consider himself a fool.

"I want to be there to see the body," he insisted.

"You fool. If you show up, the deal is off." He wondered why he suffered fools like Lester. He didn't need the money and he no longer needed the excitement and power of controlling life and death. Maybe he'd walk away from it all.

He went back to his room. It was his habit to fall into a deep sleep before a kill. He always awoke with his senses sharpened. Today sleep didn't come. He didn't trust Lester. He worked alone and suddenly he was being smothered by a wanna-be. Maybe he'd finish this job and disappear. The night he spent with Mindy played through his mind. He wondered what it would be like to sleep with the same woman night after night. Maybe he'd try it. Mindy was a giving woman and he was a taking man. Finally he relaxed and slept.

By the time he tucked himself in Michaela's closet, he had made up his mind that this would be his last job.

* * *

Mick felt free and loved. Here she stood in the midst of an art show surrounded by Bert, Hap, Peg, Gloria and Betty. She could almost feel the loneliness dripping from her body and melting at her feet. It must have been a heavy load because she felt so light. She hadn't been this content since that single bullet struck down Matthew. He'd told her to live and, like always, she'd try anything to please him. She felt him beside her tonight. She wished she could explain that to Bert but for now, it was enough that she knew Matthew was here.

"I have an idea," she said. "Why don't you all come over to my condo for a while? I promise it will be more comfortable than standing in the middle of a crowd." She saw the surprise on everyone's face. Clearly they thought she was a recluse.

"Well, it's late but we can't pass up the opportunity to prolong the good company," Hap answered.

"Count me in," Gloria said. "Can I stop and pick up something to drink?"

"That's perfect," Bert said. "I would do it but Michaela is with me. Do you all want to follow us? Betty, you'll come, won't you?" He hadn't wanted to speak directly to her but she was the only one who hadn't answered.

"She's with me and I'll refuse to take her home," Gloria laughed.

Betty was torn. Memories of museum events had flooded through her all evening. She missed Carol and the work they did together. They'd made a good team. She had floated in and out of this conversation but she knew Gloria would twist her arm when they got in the car. She'd go along and they'd forget her. If she refused, they'd remember.

Michaela loved having guests in her home. She invited everyone to help themselves to the beer and wine that Gloria brought. Peg and Gloria studied the photos she had on the wall.

"Are these all your work?" Peg asked.

"Yes."

"Is this taken in Big Bend?"

"Yes, it's a marvelous place to take photographs."

"And is this in the Guadalupe Mountains?" Gloria asked.

"Yes. I lived in Arizona so I had plenty of opportunity to travel the Southwest." Mick couldn't believe she'd just told everyone where she came from. Fear stole in as she remembered how easy it would be for someone to connect the dots. "That was a long time ago," she added.

"Isn't she talented as well as beautiful?" Bert joined them.

"Yes, she is." Gloria saw past his comment. She believed Bert may be finding love again. For his sake, she hoped so. Michaela needed love too but Gloria thought too much stood in the way. She didn't know what, but Michaela was a troubled soul.

Like Betty. Where was Betty? She looked and saw her standing alone back in the kitchen. *Well, she'd change that.* "Betty, where are you? I want you to see this picture. You're going to love it."

"I'll be there in a minute. I'm just pouring another glass of wine." A little white lie never hurt anyone, she rationalized.

Bert loved the style and comfort of Michaela's home. It showed a new side of her. Her eclectic taste was new to him. He noticed the books, a pair of brass puppy bookends, a Casablanca movie poster and an antique clock. It all spoke of cozy contentment. But why couldn't he relax? He looked at Hap and noticed the same apprehension. Was it a gender thing? The women were enthusiastically discussing art.

"I found this marvelous miniature in El Paso," Mick said. "Let me get it." She headed toward the bedroom. Gloria followed. Suddenly Mick shuddered.

"Someone just walk over your grave?" Gloria asked.

"Wow, I haven't heard that since my grandmother died. And yes, I have that feeling." Mick picked up the miniature and rushed back to the living room. Gloria paused and scanned the bedroom before following her. Although the conversation continued, Mick's enthusiasm disappeared.

Gloria and Betty were saying their goodbyes when someone rattled the door knob. Mick froze. Bert ran to the door and saw a man's face through the peephole. He frantically motioned Mick over to look. The color drained from her face as she recognized him.

"Who is it? What's wrong?" Bert asked as he motioned Hap to the door. Silence filled the room.

Michaela shook so hard she couldn't answer. She tried to remember where she'd seen that man. She knew it had something to do with Matthew. She shivered and Bert wrapped her in his arms.

"I need to check the house," Hap told everyone. "Stay in this room." A sudden noise came from the bedroom. Hap ran in to see the open back door. By the time he ran out on the deck, he saw a man running down the street. He was carrying something long that looked like a rifle but it was too far for Hap to be sure. He shouted to Peg, "Call 9-1-1."

When Bert looked back out the peephole, the man was gone. He rushed out the front door ahead of Hap. As they ran, Hap described the man he'd seen running. When they reached the street, it was empty.

"Let's go in different directions," Bert suggested.

"No, we've lost both of them. Let's stay with the women until the police come." They found

Michaela on the couch surrounded by her three caring friends.

"I'm not sure they need us," Bert said.

Hap nodded as sirens sounded in the distance.

The police spent the next hour making a report about the incident. They told Michaela there was little they could do since she had no names and nobody was hurt. They did tell her they would drive by her home at least once each shift. They would file their report in the morning and she could pick up a copy.

* * *

What a disaster! Stuck in a crowded closet with a house full of people. This was the one thing he'd never anticipated. He had watched her place for several days and no one ever came. He should never have given in to Lester's idea. He knew it never paid to hurry a hit. Now he had problems. He had a touch of claustrophobia and tended to hyperventilate in tight places. He knew Lester's plan had disaster written all over it. So he was the fool now.

Nobody came in the bedroom and he thought about leaving. He could see a sliver of the living room through the crack in the closet doors. He had already planned an escape route as an alternative to walking out the front door. A bedroom door opened onto a small deck. It was only on the second floor so a jump would suffice in an emergency. His above-average agility proved a plus in his trade.

He was planning his escape when Michaela came into the bedroom, followed by another woman. He held his breath and his senses went to full alert. She felt him there even though he remained motionless. She reminded him of a deer caught in the headlights—aware but unable to stop the catastrophe. Michaela grabbed something and ran out of the room. The other woman hesitated before she followed. He shouldn't have to wait much longer. He moved just enough to get a straighter view through the door crack.

He heard a noise at the door and saw the man look out the peephole and motion Michaela. When she froze and paled, he knew who stood on the other side of the door. That idiot Lester was checking on his work. Fury slammed him. He had to get out of the closet and away from here now. He silently slithered out of the closet and opened the back door. In his haste, he forgot to close the door. He stepped over the deck railing and swung down onto the bottom-floor deck, and hit the ground running. He had no intention of meeting Lester again. He always planned alternative escape routes. Today he had left a small kayak on the bay's edge. In the dark he could glide away unnoticed.

He pulled his kayak ashore on the south shore where he'd parked a car. He drove along Boca Chica Beach until he was in sight of the Rio Grande

River. Tonight the river was shallow, the slivered moon shed little light and no Border Patrol agents waited around the mouth of the river.

He reached Mexico and didn't look back. Maybe he'd send someone back for the car. Mindy would have to wait.

* * *

Lester knew he'd lost the man's services but he had every right to be worried. He had waited as he'd said he would but the man never came. He only wanted to see Michaela's body. Then it would be done. Unfortunately he hadn't planned an alternative if there were live people in the condo.

Now he had to face the fact that she might have seen him. He didn't know if she would recognize him if she did. So far this trip spelled failure but he'd find a way. For now, he needed to get off the island. When he drove onto the causeway, he breathed a sigh of relief. He had plenty of time to plan and this time, he'd take care of it himself.

* * *

In Tucson, sleep eluded Juan. Even Lourdes' head on his shoulder failed to calm the storm within. His apprehension had deepened since he overheard Lester's conversation, followed by his sudden trip. He'd long since stopped asking God's forgiveness for hurting his own kind—people like his beautiful wife who only wanted a better chance in life. Each time he unloaded his truck, he had to face the fact that most of these people would be caught and deported in worse condition than when they originally left. He was part of the operation that took their money and built their hopes when he knew there was so little hope for them. He wasn't just part of it. He was taking a cut and putting the money away to help his own family. Who helped those poor people he was stealing from, for that is what he was doing. He was stealing their dreams of a better life. He would burn in hell for his sins.

13

However long the night, the dawn will break

African Proverb

AFTER THE POLICE finished their reports, and Hap and Peg had gone home, Michaela walked into Bert's arms and wished she could stay there forever. She had answered so many questions, and repeated her story so many times. Did the police not believe her? She knew she'd told a convoluted story but she couldn't tell them about Matthew. She didn't know why he'd been killed but as soon as she saw the man outside her door, she understood that Matthew had a life she knew nothing about.

When they had been together, Mick felt complete. She had never questioned him, except for teasing him about his girlfriends. She had learned to live in the moment after her parents' deaths and her times with Matthew had been too precious to think of outside concerns. Now she wished she'd asked him about his life. Her memories were all she had left. She wouldn't share them with the police or anyone else, not even Bert.

She felt safe for the moment nestled in Bert's arms, but she knew she'd never be free again. She trembled at the knowledge the man had found her. Not one man, but two. In her terror at recognizing the first man's face, she'd almost forgotten the man who fled from her house. Had he been in the closet or under her bed? She didn't want to ever go back in her bedroom again. She'd have to move. Maybe just to another condo. No, she had to leave South Padre Island and her new-found friends. And Bert. She wasn't sure how she felt about him, but she trusted him. She needed that now.

Bert felt her trembling and led her to the couch, never taking his arms away. He was content to hold her while she sorted through the shock, the police reports and the answers she'd given. He knew there was more than what she told them, but he wouldn't ask. She would tell him when she was ready, and he'd be here waiting. In the meantime, as Michaela's heartbeats slowed, she started to relax. Bert wanted so much from her, but tonight he was content to be her security. The morning sun found them on the couch, arms entwined, and fast asleep.

Bert awoke first. He needed to find the bathroom and a coffee pot, in that order, but he didn't want to wake Michaela. His first thought had been that she might try to run. She had obviously run to the island.

With the double fright of the man at the door and the man in her bedroom, she'd panicked. He had to keep her here where he could protect her. How could he convince her to stay? When he couldn't wait any longer, he gently disentangled himself and tiptoed toward the bathroom.

Holding her all night with nothing but comfort on his mind was something he'd never before experienced. If he were honest, he'd have to admit he had much more than comfort on his mind, but his heart ruled and he gave her what she needed most. That was all the proof he needed to know he loved her with a love that put her needs before his. It was an experience that brought with it a sense of wonder.

The sudden cold where his warmth had been woke Michaela. She'd been in that in-between land where awareness gently nudged. She heard the bathroom door close and re-arranged herself. She'd never before slept on the couch all night snuggled up in a man's arms. Bert had kept the terror at bay but now it slammed into her. A man had been hiding here. She knew he meant her harm. She realized a chance decision to invite guests over might have saved her life—or at least saved her from whatever the man's intentions had been.

God, she had to get out of here. She jumped from the couch to go pack but when she reached the bedroom door, she froze. She couldn't go in there alone. She'd wait for Bert and then she had to convince him she needed to leave. Or maybe she could just tell him she was afraid to use her bedroom. He'd help her move everything to her living room. When he left, she'd pack and leave today.

She looked at her photographs and paintings. This time she couldn't take the time to load up everything. She'd have to leave much of her life behind. Maybe after she was gone, Bert would take her pictures to remember her. She liked the thought of him reliving their short, doomed relationship through her photography.

Bert heard her walk to the bedroom and stop. When he opened the door, he felt her terror. She couldn't force herself to step in the room. He rushed to her, took her in his arms and whispered, "It'll be all right. I'm here and I'll protect you with my life."

"No," she shouted and pushed him away. "I can't put your life at risk too."

"Michaela, we'll solve this together. I love you." My God, he'd blurted it out and that would frighten her even more. "I'm sorry. I didn't mean to . . ."

"Don't."

He'd blown it. He didn't know what to say. "Michaela . . ." His entire body pleaded with her.

Bert stunned her. It was like she'd been frozen in place. She thought of the stories she'd read of ancient Pompeii where the lava from the erupting volcano swept over and preserved the people on the spot.

"Michaela, please . . ."

She thought of ice storms and mud slides. She thought of the bombing of Hiroshima. Her mind flitted from one half-formed thought to another, anything and everything but Bert's words. She thought of movies where a person's soul stepped outside her body. That was it, she was having an out-of-body experience. Time was standing still.

Bert fought between despair and his need to protect her. The doorbell rang. Neither moved until its insistence brought Bert to life. He answered the door to find the two police officers who'd taken their statements last night.

"We're just checking on you," Officer Chavez said. "We canvassed the area last night but nobody saw anything. The two men could still be on the island or gone. We wanted to ask Ms Flanagan if she could describe the man at the door to a sketch artist."

"He did nothing wrong, but Ms Flanagan's fear and the fact that a man was in the house at the time make it too much of a coincidence," Murphy, the other officer, added.

"Yes, I could," Michaela, who hadn't moved, said as she walked toward them.

"Do you mind coming to the station this afternoon at 1:00?"

"I'll go with you," Bert squeezed her hand.

Mick hesitated but she knew she had to do this. She'd still have time to get out of town today. "Okay." The officers strained to hear her soft reply.

"Good, we'll see you there. And remember, Ms Flanagan, we are here to protect you."

"Can you come here instead?" Bert asked. Officer Chavez picked up on the worry in his voice and readily agreed.

* * *

Lester reached Tucson in time to check in with Fred. He'd driven straight through except for an hour-long nap at a rest stop. It was a long, boring drive and night time didn't help. At least it kept the poverty of the small towns hidden from view.

Although he was tired, he knew Fred needed to know he was in town. They had a run scheduled for tomorrow night and he needed to check last-minute arrangements. He'd call Juan and then he'd get some much needed sleep.

Juan was at work so he left a message.

* * *

Gloria felt like she was spending too much time back-peddling. Betty had withdrawn into herself again. Not that she could blame her. What a frightening experience. Thank God that Michaela had Bert to look after her. His feelings would be tested before this all was resolved. She'd done a lot of things in her life but this was proving to be a major challenge. However, she'd never been known as one to give up. She'd told Betty she'd pick her up for lunch tomorrow and she'd start again.

Betty wanted to enjoy life again. So many roadblocks popped up but she realized her life was much easier than poor Michaela's. Why was there so much violence in life anymore? She'd spent a lifetime with it never touching her and now it was knocking at her door again.

14

I hold it to be the inalienable right of anybody to go to hell in his own way.

Robert Frost

JUAN AND HANK'S trip was uneventful except in Juan's mind. He found it harder each time to load and unload human cargo. The hope and hopelessness seeped through every pore and by the time the evening ended, his sweat-drenched body was completely drained. He took the money from Lester but it burned a hole in his heart—or what part of his heart remained. He was fast becoming the kind of person he despised. But how did he quit without hurting Lourdes and his family?

He didn't like the look in Lester's eyes tonight. He saw an anger and a wildness that hadn't been there before. Juan wondered if it had any connection to the conversation he overheard last week.

As he drove back down the road, he met a big car headed toward the barn. In all the trips he'd made, he'd never seen another car at the barn. Was something wrong?

He dropped Hank off at his house and stopped down the street. Should he go home or should he go back? What if that had been an unmarked police car? If he went back, they could arrest him. More than likely, it was someone wanting to talk to Lester about the next leg of their business. He'd never met any of Lester's partners but he was sure he had them. It was too big an operation for one man. Juan put the car in gear and headed home. He hoped that Lourdes was in a good mood tonight.

* * *

Lester realized Michaela would probably run again. He shouldn't have left the island without finishing the job. The Mexican had created a mess and walked out. He should have anticipated that Michaela might change her routine. He forgot that the whole unfortunate mess had been of his making.

Why couldn't he pull off a drive-by shooting himself? Then he wouldn't have to deal with idiots. Everyone walked places on the island. It would be easy to pull it off on on the side streets. Too many cars moved up and down Padre Blvd. There were only two other north-south streets— Gulf and Laguna, so named by their closeness to the body of water. It would be harder to get back on Padre Blvd from Gulf so Laguna offered a better chance. He'd have to find someone to follow her activities. The street had plenty of restaurants with great bay views. Most islanders frequented one or more.

If that didn't work, he'd have to look at Plan B, which would be to grab her and take her somewhere to get rid of her. That presented more things that could go wrong. He'd go with the first plan. All he needed was someone to find out Michaela's routine. He didn't know anyone on the island so he'd have to send someone and he didn't have much time to decide. He could control his delivery team so one of them would be the obvious choice.

Hank feared that his wife would find out about Maria, so he would do whatever Lester ordered. He wasn't the sharpest knife in the drawer though. Robbie and Carlos needed money for their families but they were young and less stable. He didn't want to turn one of them loose. That left Juan, the one he trusted the least but held the biggest weapon over his head. He'd do anything to save Lourdes and his children. He'd resent it while he did it but fear would win out. Juan had been acting strange the last few days. Maybe it was time to turn the vise a little tighter.

He picked up his phone and placed the call.

"Juan, we need to meet. Usual place tonight—5 p. m." He never gave his name over the phone.

"Something wrong, Boss?"

"No, just be there at 5:00," Lester ended the call.

Juan worried the rest of the day. He'd had plans to take his kids to the park and have pizza afterwards. Now he'd have to forget about the park. He'd have the pizza delivered earlier and tell Lourdes he had a meeting. She never questioned him but he knew it was difficult for her. He wondered what she thought.

He arrived at the barn a few minutes before 5:00. He wondered if it was empty now but he wouldn't get out of his car until he saw Lester. This meeting worried him because he couldn't trust him. Lester wouldn't ask for a meeting unless something was wrong.

Lester pulled up and got out of the car. "I have a job for you," he began.

"Another truckload?"

"No, this is more important and I need someone I can trust." Lester trusted his ability to control Juan's actions but he couldn't put it like that.

"What?" A bad feeling settled in Juan's stomach.

"I want you to take a trip and do some work."

"A trip? To where?"

"South Padre Island."

"I can't go that far away. Lourdes and the children need me."

"You can, and you will."

"Why? How would I explain it to my wife?"

"That's your problem. You will go because I need you to. I want you to watch someone for a few days, that's all."

"For what reason?"

"None of your business. I need to know what someone is doing, and that's all you need to know."

"I can't," Juan said.

"You can if you want your wife to remain in this country, if you want your children to have a mother."

"But . . ."

"You will do it. I want you to leave in the morning. I'll pay your gas and your expenses plus your regular hourly rate for eight hours a day."

"I can't get vacation time that fast."

"Call in sick. Just make it happen."

Lester knew he'd get objections from Juan but he had no patience tonight. "Look, you leave in the morning and you'll get there in about fifteen or sixteen hours. I will give you the address where Michaela lives and all you have to do is keep a record of where she goes and when. Call me each night at 9:00."

"When would I come home?"

"Stay three full days. Leave the morning of the fourth day and you 'll be home to your precious family that night. If you vary this in any way, your family will never be the same. Are we clear?"

Juan nodded as he swallowed his defeat.

* * *

"You cannot leave here," Bert told her again. He had confronted Michaela and she tearfully admitted her plan to leave. He hadn't let her out of his sight all day and he planned to stay with her again tonight.

"I have to."

"Why?"

"I just have to. You don't understand."

"No, I don't and you're not about to explain, are you?" Bert hated hearing his voice rise but he had almost reached his limit.

"I don't owe you anything. Certainly not an explanation of my life." Anger and frustration lit her eyes. "Leave me alone. I never asked for your help."

"I know and I wish you had. I'm here for you, can't you see that?"

"Did I ask you to be?" Michaela fought to avoid throwing herself in his arms and crying till her fear went away. He was trying so hard to help but she couldn't accept it. She couldn't, and wouldn't, put him in the middle. He had no idea what that man was capable of.

"Michaela, my dear, please . . ." Bert changed tactics since anger wasn't working. He'd plead and beg if that's what it took. He'd follow her wherever she went.

Silence was the only answer she could give. If she spoke, she'd cry. Her anger was spent and God, she was weary. She just wanted God to make everything go away. She wanted life like it was before Matthew was killed. She forgot Bert and he felt it. He stepped back, defeated.

If I leave, she'll let me go, he told himself. No, he would stay here and give her space but he wouldn't give up.

Mick sank into a chair. She wanted him to leave and she wanted him to stay. She welcomed his anger more than his pleading. She really wanted him to take charge and make it all go away.

Bert knelt in front of her and took her hand. "I'm here," he whispered. "And I'm staying."

Her tears fell on his hand.

* * *

Lourdes' anger poured over Juan. He was defenseless, to tell her the truth would ruin them and to lie was doing the same.

"Are you going alone or not?" Lourdes could think of only one reason he'd take a trip without her and it had nothing to do with work. She didn't believe that excuse for a minute.

"It's for work."

"Do I look that stupid? You don't travel for work and you know it. Why don't you just admit it? You're tired of supporting a family or is it just that I'm not enough for you anymore?"

"Lourdes, you, Jorge and Rosita are my life. You're why I'm doing this work." His pleading fell on deaf ears.

"Go, and I don't care if you ever come back."

Juan stood motionless for what seemed like hours since she'd stomped out of the room. He knew he wouldn't be welcome in their bed tonight. He had no choice and he saw no way out. If she only knew how much he hated this job, she'd be comforting him. He decided to leave now—he wouldn't even pack clothes because he couldn't face her again. He looked in on Rosita and Jorge and their sleep of innocence broke his heart. Everything he loved and worked for was in this house. He walked into the kitchen to make a cup of coffee for the road. He rubbed his hands over the cabinets he'd made for Lourdes last Christmas. As the coffee brewed he pictured a happier Lourdes herding her family to the table for dinner. He could almost smell her homemade salsas.

He poured his coffee and silently shut the door behind him. In his truck, he texted "I love you," to his wife.

Juan headed out of town thinking about Lourdes and her desire to become a citizen. With nothing more than a high school education, he didn't consider himself smart enough to solve the government's problems but he felt she was an asset to any country. Rosita and Jorge were fortunate to have her for their mother. Surely there was a way better than hiding the truth by smuggling other illegals. If God was truly listening to his prayers, shouldn't He be doing something? No, it wasn't fair to blame God. He and Lourdes created this problem all on their own. Lester simply took advantage of it.

He drove and thought until sleepiness became a problem. He pulled into a Stripes parking lot in Laredo and slept for a couple hours. He bought a cup of coffee and a candy bar to get him the rest of the way. It was mid-afternoon when he crossed the causeway. Sunlight glistened on the bay and a pirate ship caught his eye. He'd been here once as a child but he remembered nothing except playing on the beach. He'd promised Lourdes a vacation here but time or money was always an issue. No wonder she was furious. He was going alone to the place she'd only dreamed about. He'd make it up to her. He'd take home some souvenirs and plan their trip while he was here.

He saw a Denny's and his stomach growled. He needed lunch and then he'd find his hotel. He had the rest of the day to wander around but he needed food and sleep first. If the hotel didn't have a room ready, he'd nap in the truck.

When he pulled into the parking lot, he checked his phone. Nothing from Lourdes.

By late afternoon, he'd napped an hour and was ready to check into his hotel room. He asked the man at the desk where he could get a good taco. The man said he liked Manuel's in Port Isabel but they closed at 2:00. Juan decided to grab a Coke at Whataburger and start his work early. He looked at the map that Lester had given him, found the street and drove by the woman's condo. He couldn't remember her name but he knew it was an unusual one. He dug through Lester's papers again until he found it. Michaela, no last name, but he did have a photograph. She was pretty but when he thought of beauty, he thought of Lourdes.

He'd never done this sort of thing before and had to rely on his common sense and memories of movies and cop TV shows. When he parked down the street from her condo, he had no idea whether or not she was home. He realized he could wait for hours. What did cops do when they needed a bathroom? The movies never dealt with such basic needs as hunger, bathroom breaks and sleep. He figured he'd most likely experience all three.

He was right. By the time the woman's garage door opened, he was desperate for two of the three. At least he'd had enough sleep earlier so that wasn't an issue. A man took the driver's seat after he held the passenger door for the woman. Lester hadn't said anything about a man living with her, but then he was sure Lester left out a lot. The couple backed out, turned toward the bay and then south. He waited a minute and pulled out behind them. There were no other cars so he lagged a couple of blocks behind. They stopped at a restaurant on the bay. La Hacienda. Good, he was already hungry for spicy salsa. He waited about five minutes before entering the restaurant. The couple sat at a table along the window with two other women. Juan was the only person alone and he felt awkward. He looked toward the bar but he didn't want a drink. Although he liked a Corona with dinner, he never drank when he had work to do. After he'd visited the bathroom, the waiter seated him.

Betty watched the man sit down at a corner table. She felt sorry for anyone eating alone. In her mind it was the ultimate in loneliness. Thank God she was in company she was learning to enjoy. She wanted to ease Michaela's fear but didn't know how, except for keeping her company. It felt good to care about someone other than herself. Gloria's laugh pulled her back into the conversation. Gloria and Bert entertained Michaela with one story after another. They watched the sun bathe the sky and bay in shades of orange and mauve.

"Michaela, would you mind if I took over your kitchen tomorrow?" Bert laughed at the surprise on her face.

"For what?"

"To fix a dinner for the four of us tomorrow evening. Does that work for the two of you?" He asked Gloria and Betty.

"Can you cook?" Gloria asked.

"Can I cook? I'll show you tomorrow, and then you'll never again doubt my talent in the kitchen."

"And what will the menu hold?" Gloria wanted to know.

"Ah, you'll have to come hungry and find out."

They joked with Bert as they left the restaurant. Betty stopped to visit the restroom. When she walked past the dining room, the man she had noticed earlier had left.

15

Being deeply loved by someone gives you strength, while loving someone deeply gives you courage.

Lao Tzu

JUAN'S DAYS DRAGGED but he shadowed Michaela as closely as possible. The man apparently never left her side. They shopped at the grocery store and CVS together. In the afternoon two men arrived. One carried a briefcase. Their visit lasted nearly an hour. In the evening, the two women they'd met last night arrived. They stayed several hours so Juan guessed they had been invited for dinner.

He had plenty of time to question Lester's motives. The woman's life seemed ordinary. What was Lester's interest in her? From Juan's experience, it wouldn't be anything good. He thought about how ordinary most people are—at least from what others see. He wondered how this woman's life connected her to Lester? Did he know some secret about her like he knew about Lourdes? Juan knew that Lester held the power to destroy his wife. He hoped it wasn't the same with Michaela.

The second morning, the man with the briefcase returned but this time a police officer accompanied him. Their visit was shorter than yesterday—thirty minutes or so. Seeing the police gave Juan a jolt. Maybe God was sending a sign that Lester was up to no good. If he meant her harm, did watching her make him a part of whatever Lester plotted? He'd parked a block away today. She lived on a short street and Juan felt he was too obvious but he didn't know where else to go. He called for Lourdes several times but she wasn't answering. He hoped his messages softened her heart and let her know he was missing her. He wanted to hear Rosita's and Jorge's voices. He wanted to be home.

The third day dragged even longer because nobody left and nobody visited all day. In the evening they went to dinner again. They met the same two ladies and an older couple at a place called PadreRitaGrill. Juan avoided the bar again and asked for a table in a corner. The open dining area made it hard for him to fade in the background. As the tables filled, he became more comfortable. He'd loved to be close enough to hear their conversation, but no way would he take that risk.

* * *

When the waiter brought their drinks, Betty looked around and her eyes focused on the man all alone in a corner table. "That's the same man I saw at La Hacienda the other night," she pointed him out to the others.

"He has good taste in restaurants," Bert commented. He saw concern in Hap Lynch's eyes, but he didn't want to alarm Michaela. He steered the conversation away from Betty's comment. Michaela was busy pointing out menu items to Peg.

When they left the restaurant Bert and Hap lagged behind the women. "What do you think?" Bert asked.

"He's still here. I'll watch to see if he follows us."

Bert caught up with Michaela and gallantly kissed each woman's hand. He put his arm around Michaela and ushered her into the car. He wanted to get away before the man came out.

Hap took his time buckling his seatbelt and fiddling with his GPS. "What's wrong, Hap?" Peg asked.

"Not sure. I want to wait a few minutes to see if the man Betty pointed out follows Michaela."

"What makes you think he would? He's probably a man who's here on business or he's single."

"I hope you're right. I wouldn't think anything about it, except that Betty saw him the other night."

"Could just be a coincidence."

"I hope you're right."

The door opened. Two couples walked out followed by the man in question. Hap took note of the car he drove and took down the license number before he drove out of the parking lot in the direction of Michaela's house. Hap followed. The man drove to a hotel and went inside.

"Maybe I was wrong," he told Peg as he turned the car around.

* * *

Juan had been nervous during dinner. He saw one of the women nod toward him as she said something to the rest of the group. One of the women—the one he hadn't seen before—turned and looked in his direction. I told Lester I'd be no good at this. He had no idea what to do. It would look even stranger if he left without eating. He decided to enjoy his meal. He waited a little longer before following them out of the restaurant. He noticed someone in one of the cars at the end of the lot but it was dark and he couldn't tell who it was. He decided to go back to his hotel instead of checking the woman's house. When a car pulled out of the lot behind him, he thought he'd made the right choice.

The next morning Juan drove by the woman's house but didn't stop. It was early and he was anxious to get home. He stopped at a t-shirt shop to buy souvenirs. He found a pair of dolphin earrings for Lourdes and shirts for the kids. He hoped Lourdes had forgiven him by now. He needed her. It had been a long three days and he had a bad feeling about the whole job. He hoped he wouldn't have to see Lester until tomorrow. By the time he reached San Antonio, he'd already received two texts from Lester. He ignored them.

By the time he pulled in his driveway, he'd convinced himself that Lourdes would be happy to see him. He was sure she missed him as much as he missed her. He was wrong. The cold shoulder treatment continued and he spent the rest of the night on the couch. He didn't answer any of Lester's messages.

After Jorge and Rosita left for school the next morning, he tried to talk to Lourdes.

"I brought you and the children a gift," he told her.

"Don't think you can bribe me."

"I love you, sweetheart, and I need your love."

The sincerity and loneliness in his voice reached into her. She couldn't punish him for what he might have done. Maybe he'd told her the truth. She knew he loved her and, God knows, she loved him with all her heart. He had always taken care of her, loved her and treated her special. It was selfish to punish him anymore.

Tears rolled down her cheeks as his arms enveloped her. All was right in Juan's world—at least for this moment.

He wanted to stay like this forever but he had to work and then meet Lester.

"I'll be home as early as I can tonight. Will you please fix Carne Guisada for dinner?"

"Of course I will."

* * *

Fury ate at Lester all day. How dare Juan not return his texts. He'd not called either night. He better have something to report or he'd be sorry. If Juan thought he could cross him, he had plenty to learn.

He'd had a rough couple of days anyway. Fred nagged at him constantly. He was making the guy rich and his only reward was complaining. So he'd brought up Matthew again. That was because they were still in danger from Michaela. He couldn't tell Fred he'd found her or that she'd seen and recognized him. By the time Juan showed up that evening, Lester had worked himself into a rant.

"How dare you. I told you to call me. See this," he shook a piece of paper. "This is a letter I'm taking to the immigration authorities. You've pushed me too far this time."

"Slow down, sir, I did what you wanted."

"I can't trust you anymore. We're through and your wife is going back to Mexico."

Juan detested this threat. He'd heard it so many times but it instilled enough fear to get its intended response. "You can trust me. I found the woman and followed her for three days."

Lester's body told him to calm down. The pain between his shoulder blades hit again. He took a deep breath and waited for it to subside.

Juan watched Lester's face flush and sweat. "Are you all right?"

The question renewed his anger but he had to ignore it.

He nodded, "Just give me a minute."

"Can I do something?"

"Wait." Lester tried to hide his pain but it wasn't possible with Juan hovering over him.

Juan waited. Lester's breathing finally slowed and his face returned to normal. If he died, I'd be free...Forgive me, Jesus. I'm sorry. His roller-coaster emotions ended in guilt. Could he really ask Jesus to forgive him for wishing death on a person? Was it a sin to think it if he did nothing to make it come true? He should ask his priest but he couldn't admit it, even to him. Or maybe he didn't want to hear his answer. *How many times can God forgive me? I think I've gone through my share.*

"Okay. I'm okay now."

"Thank God," Juan's voice was little more than a whisper.

"So, what did you find out?"

"She doesn't leave her home much. You didn't tell me a man lived with her."

"I didn't know."

"Wherever they went, they were together."

"What did they do?"

"They went out to dinner with friends two nights and had the same friends over the other night. Other than a trip to the grocery store, they stayed home."

"That's all?"

"That's it. It was a long three days."

"I don't care about that," Lester chewed on his fingernail. "You didn't see anything else?"

"No . . . wait. Two men visited the first day. One guy had a briefcase."

"Who were they?"

"I don't know. Ordinary looking guys, except the guy with the briefcase was back the next day with a police officer. They went inside both days."

"That's all you saw?"

"Yes."

"Did they see you?"

"No." Juan figured a little white lie wouldn't hurt his already blackened soul.

* * *

Every night Mick promised herself she'd leave tomorrow but by the light of day, Bert never left her side.

He would plan vacations for the two of them, researching photo ops and building their dream world. They talked about a region's history and culture. She appreciated his love of music and architecture. They watched classic movies to study the architecture of the time period. Day after day, he birthed a longing in her. In her mind she pictured them walking the Great Wall of China, capturing the color of the Greek Islands dotting the sea, riding a hot-air balloon to see giraffes' faces up close or zip lining through the rain forests of Costa Rica. Bert kept her fear at bay until the night.

He'd started sleeping with her but had yet to turn comfort into something more. She longed to explore love but for now she was content.

Bert was anything but. By day, he fell more in love with Michaela's creative, inquiring mind. When night came, he struggled to maintain control. He wanted much more from her than just sex, but still he found it physically painful to lie beside her and do nothing more than hold her. Surely he'd given her enough comfort by now but she showed no signs of desire. Some nights he resented her neediness until guilt exposed his selfishness. How could he think only of himself when danger threatened the woman he loved?

* * *

"You're obsessed with her." Fred wondered why Lester couldn't see how it was changing him.

"I will take care of it and it will be over. I'll be free of her and Matthew." Lester had asked Fred to meet him.

"You will never be free as long as you chase problems that don't exist. You've let this imagined crisis weaken you and your organization."

"Nothing is weakened, unless it's you." Lester hated that Fred knew how to push his buttons. He had to get out of here and take matters in his own hands. He had given Fred one last chance to see reason. "I'm outta here. Get your hands dirty and see what the real problems are." He stormed out of the barn.

"Come back here now." Fred yelled as Lester slammed his truck door and tore out of the drive.

Lester made an immediate decision and swiped his arm across his sweaty face. He headed to South Padre Island without a change of clothes. He carried his gun and that was all he needed.

After his anger wore off, he slowed down. The highway was crawling with cops and border-patrol vehicles tonight. He had business to take care of. He called Juan and left a message that he had to go out of town for a few days. If a load became available, he'd let him know. He pulled off the road in Fort Stockton for a short nap but that only took him to San Antonio. He found a Motel 6 but tossed and turned the rest of the night.

16

When justice is done, it is a joy to the righteous but terror to evildoers.

Proverbs 23:25

JUAN WOKE UP for a bathroom break and noticed that he had a message from Lester. Listening proved to be a mistake because it kept him awake the rest of the night. Lester left town and something in Juan's gut told him that he had gone to South Padre Island. The suddenness of the trip and the tone of his voice convinced Juan that Lester was going because of the woman. He meant her harm. No other explanation made sense.

Juan had thought back to the first time he'd met Lester. He'd been harsh, threatening and showed a wide streak of cruelty but he hadn't been angry. When had that changed? When had anger replaced common sense? He thought Lester was far more dangerous now than before.

Lourdes woke with the alarm. Juan had made a decision that he knew would upset her. She had the right to know the whole story. "I have to go," he told her. "I have to try to stop something I may have made possible. I can't tell you now but when I get home, you'll understand."

"But, Juan, you can't tell me that and then leave me here knowing nothing. Are you in trouble?"

"I could be but I'm more worried about losing you. I love you and the children but I've made a terrible mistake. Please don't ask me more now. Please just love me and be here when I get home."

"You are worrying me to death but you know I'll be here. I love you too, you silly fool, but I'm dying of curiosity. So go, before I tie you down and beat it out of you." Lourdes' attempt at a laugh fell flat as tears filled her eyes.

While she went to wake the children, Juan threw a few things in a duffel bag and he was ready to leave by the time everyone made it into the kitchen.

"I'll make you some breakfast," she told him.

"Just a cup of coffee," he answered as he grabbed a couple cookies from the cookie jar.

"I want a cookie, too," Rosita clapped her hands.

"You have cereal, little one," he told her. "Maybe your mama will give you a cookie after school."

"Will you, Mama?"

"If you're a good girl in school today." Lourdes loved Rosita's enthusiasm.

"Are you leaving, Papá?" Jorge asked.

"Just for a few days. I want you to take care of your mama and your little sister while I'm gone, okay?"

"Sure, Papá, I will."

Juan kissed Lourdes and headed out the door before he could change his mind.

Lourdes remained apprehensive all day and by night, worry tightened its grip. Something was changing in their lives. She could feel it in her bones. Whatever Juan would tell her when he came back would not be as terrible as the stories her imagination were spinning. She didn't believe for a minute that he could be selling drugs or be involved with the cartel. God knows plenty of men gave in to the financial pressure. She'd worried about the extra money he brought home, but it was easier to just accept their good fortune. She prayed day and night that everything would be all right. For now, she needed to keep her fears hidden from the children.

* * *

Gloating wasn't Gloria's style, but with the success of her efforts to help Betty and Mick, she gave in to it. When Hap had first approached her, she thought it was beyond her but in reality, both women just needed attention and something to focus on other than their problems. It had been a stroke of genius to ask them to help each other. Whether or not she could take credit, it was working. Betty was waking up with a purpose everyday and Mick was learning to trust people. Bert turned out to be an added bonus. They were perfect for each other and they deserved happiness. Gloria's perceptive personalty had been hewn from the rocks of experience. She was witnessing the blossoming that centered peoples' lives.

An evening of celebration was in order. She'd call and arrange dinner at Pelican Station tomorrow evening. She'd invite Hap and Peg too.

* * *

Matthew had reached into Mick's soul again last night.

"You need to tell Bert about that night."

"I know I should but I can't," Mick spoke aloud.

"He loves you and he wants to protect you. He can't if you don't give him honesty."

"Are you really here, Matthew, or are you just part of my imagination?"

This time there was no answer but Mick felt his presence and he spoke the truth. The blanket of calmness that followed told her that Matthew was pleased. She would do as he asked, to please him and to build trust with Bert.

In the morning over breakfast that was her promise to herself. It was harder than she thought.

First, it was tough to relive and second, Bert kept interrupting her.

"What did he do for a living? Why would anyone want to kill him? Could it have been accidental? Did you see the shooter? "The questions jumbled her anxiety-ridden brain. By the time she finished, she had laid out the complete story and he had promised to not question her anymore.

Bert may have agreed to not ask direct questions but he was researching on the Internet within minutes. He read the coverage of the shooting, the op-ed pieces on who was responsible, Matthew's obituary and sundry other documents. He found no more information and apparently the police had simply closed the case. He suspected Matthew wasn't the perfect creature Michaela thought he was but there was nothing to suggest he was involved in something illegal.

"Michaela, I can't be worried every day about you leaving. I will do everything I can to protect you but you have to promise me you won't leave. There has to be someone who knows why Matthew was killed. I want to find out so we understand if you're really in danger. Maybe it was a random shooting and the two of you were in the wrong place." Bert didn't for a minute believe that but he wanted her to.

"No, I feel it deep down inside, I felt it from the man at the door that night. Bert. I would give anything for you to be right. How about I make a deal with you? I won't leave until you've exhausted all of your efforts. Then we will talk."

"That's fair enough, my precious one." Bert would keep trying the rest of his life if it kept her by his side. "Now that we've settled that, what would you like to do today.?"

"I'd like to visit the Kingfisher Gallery first. I've talked to Sandy Margret about displaying some of my photos. I can't do it yet, but she gives me hope."

"That's what we'll do. How does she give you hope?"

"She's grown her business from the ground up. She's enthusiastic and has managed to create a good life for herself. She likes to work with local artists, too."

"How about a drive up the beach afterwards?"

"That sounds wonderful but can we work in time to stop at the bookstore first?"

"We have a plan," Bert smiled.

* * *

Lester wanted to get this done. The longer he thought, the more obstacles he discovered. He decided the simplest approach was to follow her and the first time he saw a clear opportunity with an easy getaway he'd do it. Michaela and the man with her were probably expecting another attempt inside her home. No way she'd expect someone to fire a shot at her out in the open. It wouldn't be a drive by because if she'd told the man about Matthew, he might be on the lookout for that. No, he'd hang around wherever she went out and if the opportunity arose, he'd take it. He was sick and tired of it all.

He rented a car in Harlingen—a white Ford Taurus. He couldn't believe his good fortune when the rental agency sent him out to pick up his car on his own. No one was in sight, so he stole a license plate from another rental company's lot and put in on the Taurus. He had parked his car in the airport's long-term rental lot. He'd return the car at night, wander around the airport for a while and then get his own car.

He waited all day until late evening before he saw Michaela. Wherever they'd gone, they'd made a day of it. The man was still with her. Lester waited an hour before returning to his hotel room. He picked up some snacks on the way. He set his alarm for 7:00. He felt certain they wouldn't go out before then.

Juan arrived on the island after dark. He stopped at Stripes, picked up a couple of tacos and some iced tea, and rented a hotel room. He chose a different hotel than before because he didn't want Lester to see him tonight. He knew his presence would send him into a rage. Juan hoped he was wrong about his boss, but he knew he wasn't. He'd wake up early and check the other hotel. If he was lucky, he'd find his car.

He called Lourdes to tell her he loved her and he'd be home as soon as possible. He avoided answering her questions and after a few minutes, she quit asking. She talked instead about Jorge and Rosita. Although Juan's heart ached for his family, he fell asleep easily,

Betty awoke early and midway through her shower, realized she was singing. Lord, how long had it been since she'd felt like singing? She had lots to do today and looked forward to dinner with her friends. She thought of Carol Flores. She missed her and could never forget her terrible death but her new friends were proof that life goes on. If Carol had lived, she might never have become good friends with Hap and Peg. Funny how acquaintances become friends. She had known Gloria for years but never spent that much time with her. And, of course, Bert wouldn't be there for Michaela when she needed him. It was so obvious that they were good for each other. She hoped it worked out for them.

She decided to celebrate her happiness by spending the morning shopping. She wanted to wear a new outfit tonight.

Hap looked forward to the evening but worry still cast its shadow. Peg left the worrying to Hap and spent her day working on her next book.

17

The truth of crime lies not with the victim but with the witness.

R. Scott Baker, Hatatian Exhortations

AFTER A SHORT wait in the bar, a waiter seated Gloria's party of six. Mick and Gloria had the best view of the bay and the causeway. Bert and Betty secured the seats with their back to the wall. Hap and Peg ended up with partial views of the bay and the entrance. *I couldn't have planned it any better*, Bert thought

"I think we're all ready to celebrate," Gloria beamed. "I'm just not sure if it's happiness or our visit to the bar."

"You're never one to beat around the bush, are you?" Hap laughed.

"Tell it like it is, Hap."

"I want to thank all of you," Mick began. "I'm still afraid but now it's only a shadow trailing me. When I first came to the island, I felt I'd never be safe again, but tonight I feel protected."

"I don't know why you were so afraid but I'm happy to be part of the cure," Betty answered. "I suspect Bert has been the main reason."

"You flatter me, Betty," Bert patted her hand.

"Well, we're way too serious for a celebration. Let's toast our good fortune." Gloria raised her glass. With the serious comments behind them, they settled into lighthearted conversation. Bert held Mick's hand until their food arrived. Her hunger for his touch was almost stronger than the emptiness in her stomach. She still experienced a little bolt of shock whenever she realized how much his presence meant to her. He had entered her life when she so badly needed someone and she would be forever grateful to him. She found it difficult to not be serious tonight because the people here with her had helped her move past her fear.

* * *

Lester had waited all day but now he couldn't believe his good fortune. It would be so much easier to escape since they'd left the island. He'd spent much of the day trying to figure out a way to get off the island after the hit. He knew the causeway would be blocked almost immediately. Now he didn't have to worry.

He looked up a map of Port Isabel on his phone and studied it while Mick and her group were in the restaurant. If he headed down Garcia, he could turn on any of the side streets, do some zigzagging and hopefully dodge the police. He thought about dumping the car but considered that a last resort. If he planned it right, nobody would notice his car anyway. His acid reflux was giving him fits again. The sooner this was done, the better.

He thought about Fred and their business. He knew Fred would take a while to cool down but after he did, their partnership should still work smoothly. With Michaela out of the way, he'd urge Fred to take on more business. He loved the violence in Mexico because it was so good for business. He chewed a couple of Tums and told himself he'd take his medicine more regularly when this was over. He debated whether to stay in the car or walk away from it. Both options carried advantages and disadvantages.

Juan sat in his car. He wasn't close enough to see Lester's features but he knew that his anger would be building the longer he waited. He could almost see the sweat breaking out on Lester's forehead and he'd bet he was feeling sick. Juan was feeling the stress, too. He had opened his eyes to the truth today. Lester intended to kill the woman. Nothing happened to make him see this but he knew it was true. He only hoped he could do something to prevent it.

He prayed and he planned what he would do in different scenarios. His success seemed doubtful under every one. Maybe God would hear him now. If he could save the woman's life, would that make up for all the truckloads of illegals he'd carried across the border? What was it the Old Testament said—something about an eye for an eye? He wondered if that's the way God judged people's actions. How many truckloads would it take to equal saving one life? It was far more complex than he could figure out.

They had been in the restaurant over an hour. Juan knew he needed to get out of the car but he didn't want Lester to see him. He counted sixteen people outside the restaurant but he could think of no way to get anywhere near them. He got out of the car, pulled a hat down over his head, hunched his shoulders and wandered over toward Dirty Al's Seafood Market.

By the time Gloria's party left the restaurant, it was dark. The tiny sliver of a moon did little to light the sky. Several groups of people lingered around the restaurant looking at the bay, making plans and saying goodnight to friends. As Michaela stepped outside, a lady's laughter rang out. It startled Mick and she reached for Bert. He put his arm around her shoulder. "Look at all the stars tonight," Gloria said. "I love it that in Texas we get to see the Big Dipper all year long."

Mick broke away from Bert and walked over to see where Gloria was pointing. "I see it. It always takes me back to my childhood. I loved it then and I still do."

"Me too. I always wanted to learn more about the constellations but I've never seemed to have the time," Gloria told her.

The others drifted their way. Out of the corner of her eye, Betty saw a man walking from the parking lot. Everyone else was going out to their cars but he was coming in. He must have forgotten something, she thought. The gulls were quiet this time of night and traffic on the causeway was minimal. It was the kind of night made for star-gazing. None of them knew much beyond the Big Dipper and Little Dipper but they had fun anyway,

Lester was ready, his .45 in hand, but he couldn't get a clear shot. He guessed he was twenty-five yards from where Michaela stood. At that distance, he should still be able to accurately do the job.

Juan kept one eye on Lester. He felt rather than saw that he had his gun ready. He hoped he'd be able to see the barrel in time. He inched closer to the woman's group. They were still gazing at the sky.

Betty turned and caught sight of him. She couldn't see his face but warning bells sounded in her brain. She motioned to Bert. He left Michaela's side to see what she wanted. Hap saw Betty motioning and he discreetly moved toward her.

Lester saw his opening. He had a clear view of Michaela's back. He raised his gun.

Juan dove in front of Michaela a split second before the gun fired. He fell as screams erupted. Bert lunged for Michaela and pushed her to the ground. He covered her body with his. Hap pulled Peg away, pushed her down and grabbed Gloria. Where was Betty? Where did the shot come from?

Betty saw the man go down. Someone had to help him. She ran to him and sank to her knees beside him. "Are you okay?" She knew he wasn't by the blood pooling around him. She nervously dialed 9-1-1, before tending to him. She found his pulse—faint, but there. He was alive. She pushed his hat off his face and froze. It was the man who followed them before.

"Hap," she whispered. "He's alive and we've seen him before."

Hap told Peg and Gloria to stay put as he crawled to Betty. No more shots had been fired. He looked around but saw no one. The parking lot was almost empty. As he turned to face Betty and the man, he heard the sirens.

Bert couldn't tell who was shaking the most— Michaela or him. He didn't dare move. Whatever else happened, he was protecting her. He'd heard no more shots.

The man murmured and Betty bent to hear. "Lourdes, tell her . . ." He drifted away as if those three words took all the energy in his body.

Was he still breathing? "Hap, do you think . . ."

"Let's keep him quiet. He's still with us."

"Jorge . . ."

"Save your energy," Hap told him.

Betty took his hand, shocked at its coldness. Was that a bad sign? Where were the police? It seemed like the sirens had been sounding forever and the police station was only blocks away. Time stood still.

"Ro . . . si . . ." His breath faded.

Hap stood up as the ambulance arrived. He motioned toward the man. "We'll take it from here. An officer will be here in a minute." The EMTs rushed to the victim.

The others stood up as two police cars arrived. Mick leaned into Bert as she looked at the man who had saved her life. "Please God, let him live."

"Stay here and don't move," an officer addressed them. They were scoping out the parking lot. With guns pulled, they began to check the few cars still in the lot. A small crowd had gathered at the door of the restaurant, customers and wait staff. "The rest of you, please go back inside. We'll talk to you in a few minutes. We need to secure the area."

"Over here," one of the officers yelled. The other officers ran to him. In the light from his flashlight, they saw a man sagging down in the driver's seat, his head against the steering wheel. The barrel of a gun glinted in the light.

Eleven hundred miles away, Lourdes was startled awake. A cold sweat drenched her body.

18

That which does not kill us makes us stronger.

Friedrich Nietzsche

"IS THE MAN alive?" Peg asked Hap as he returned from the police station.

"Yes, but it's still touch and go."

It had been well after midnight before the police finished all their questions last night. No one knew the victim or the shooter. The police had sent them home.

Detective Rachel Vasquez had not been officially assigned to the case yet but the minute she heard Hap had been involved, she wanted it. She would definitely be assigned to it if the victim died. The shooter had died at the scene, so even if the victim died, there was little need for a prolonged investigation. The department's budget was tight. They would work hard to find where the victim was from, but only a cursory effort to establish motive.

Rachel knew Hap wouldn't rest until he uncovered the whole story. She'd do everything in her power to help. She owed her career as the department's lead detective to him. She called him the next morning and asked him to come to the station.

The victim was still alive. The shooter was not. No identities had been established yet. The shooter's car had been a rental with the wrong license plates. The Harlingen police were checking with the airlines and the rental agency at the airport.

Neither Michaela nor Bert went to bed. They spent the night on the couch, talking and cuddling. Occasionally they napped. The next morning neither could remember a word of their conversation.

Bert made coffee and they drank it in silence. They didn't want to leave each other but no words could drown out the horror of the night before. The coffee seemed to calm them and they went to bed and slept until mid-afternoon. When he awoke, Bert went to the kitchen, took some eggs from the refrigerator and began to make breakfast.

Michaela stayed in bed, thinking of Matthew. Were either of those men Matthew's killer? If they both died, how would she ever find out? She was no longer sure she wanted to know the "whys and wherefores" of his death.

Deep down in her heart, she suspected he had been involved in something he didn't want her to know about. She would honor that and never ask questions. For her, he would remain a shining hero.

He had come back to help her even after his death and that kind of love deserved respect. She felt him now, asking her to throw her fears away and move on with her life. She reached for her bathrobe, slid it over her shoulders and padded in her bare feet into the kitchen. Her stomach reacted to the aroma of eggs and bacon.

"This food comes with a price," Bert wrapped his arms around her.

"And what would that be?"

"A lifetime commitment."

"All because I like bacon?" Mick wanted to prolong this conversation. She'd known she wanted to spend her life with him. Now it was music to her ears to hear him making that commitment.

"Take it or leave it."

"What happened to Mr. Gallant?"

"He died from failure to act. The new me intends to live." Bert held his breath. This was it. When he saw the man throw himself in front of Michaela and then heard the shot, something clicked. He'd wait no longer.

"Bert . . ."

"Think hard before you hesitate too long. I can't live without your commitment any longer. And the eggs and bacon are getting cold."

"And I'm hungry."

"Is that a 'yes'?"

"Is this a proposal?"

"Yep, we can celebrate later with a fancy dinner and fine wine."

"I'm fine with eggs and bacon with coffee." Tears spilled over as she smiled.

* * *

Rachel gave Hap a copy of the official police report.

Juan Cortez, the victim, received a single bullet wound in his chest. The shooter, Lester Shockley, died of a massive heart attack. Both men were from Tucson, Arizona.

Juan Cortez, a married man with two children, was recovering from his wounds, The bullet had missed his heart and arteries by a hair's width. One lung and kidney sustained serious damage. He had been transferred to a hospital in Tucson.

There were no family members or known employers to identify Shockley. His body would be cremated and his ashes held in case some one came forward.

"I'll keep digging into it," she told Hap. "I could use your help with some research."

"I'll call Elena, too."

"I knew you would. She provided some valuable information in the Flores investigation."

"Plus she finds stuff ten times faster than I do," Hap pictured Elena engrossed in her iPad.

* * *

Juan's first thought was that he was dead but then he wouldn't be in pain, would he? His chest was on fire, his head ached and he couldn't open his eyes. He tried to move one arm but it was tied down. Had he been captured? What had happened to him? He floated in and out of awareness, with the pain overpowering his brain. He couldn't remember anything.

"Shhh," the nurse quieted his moans. "You're going to be all right."

Juan tried to ask the voice where he was but his mouth didn't work.

"Don't try to talk. You've been shot and you have to be calm. You're in Valley Baptist Hospital in Brownsville."

Juan felt a stick and nothing else until he awoke again. He had no concept of time. His chest was still on fire but his brain was a little less foggy. He'd been somewhere for a reason. The details lay just beyond his grasp. If he were alive, he should remember something. Soon . . .

His life was a cycle of pain, someone quieting him, a shot and oblivion.

A male voice aroused him this time. "Juan, I'm Dr. Garcia. I've been taking care of you. We removed a bullet from your chest. You are going to be in pain for awhile but you're going to be all right."

Juan sensed his own restlessness but he couldn't wake up, or at least he couldn't open his eyes. Maybe he was awake or maybe it was all a dream. The pain in his chest assured him it was no dream - unless it was a nightmare.

"Juan, you're still in ICU because we need to monitor your lung and kidney functions. You'll be here another few days. Once we feel you are stabilized, we'll send you home to Tucson. We'll be transferring you to Carondelet-St. Mary's Hospital. You'll be closer to your wife and family."

Lourdes stepped into the room and the doctor motioned for her to stay silent. He gave Juan a shot and ushered her out the door. "Are you Mrs. Cortez?"

"Yes. Is my Juan going to be all right?"

"Yes, but he received significant damage to his lung and kidney. He's going to have a long road to recovery."

"What can I do?"

"Just be here for him. He'll be in the hospital for several weeks and then his Tucson doctors will probably find a rehab center for him."

"Why can't I take him home?"

"Mrs. Cortez, his injuries were critical. He's improving but he will need medical care for some time."

"When can I see him?"

"When he shows signs of waking up, we'll call you. Why don't you get a bite to eat or get some rest in the waiting room?"

Lourdes stormed Heaven as she waited. Later that evening, peace washed over her and she knew God had answered her prayers. Juan would be all right and whatever he wanted to confess to her would only strengthen their marriage. After all, they'd been through so much together.

Two days later by Lourdes' calendar, she sat by his bed. He was still in a coma. By Juan's calendar, he had spent an eternity somewhere between pain and sleep. Sometimes he almost reached the surface, but the pain would stop him cold. Today, as he hovered on the edge, his restlessness reached a fever pitch.

"Juan, my darling husband, I'm here with you. I love you." Lourdes had convinced the doctor to let her sit with him at thirty-minute intervals.

Did he feel or see her? One moment he felt his body rise up to touch her, but the next he merely heard a sound. Her hand touched his. Peace came with that touch. His Lourdes loved him.

EPILOGUE

Never believe that a few caring people can't change the world. For indeed, that's all who ever have.

Margaret Mead

FOUR MONTHS LATER, Rachel called Hap and asked that he and Bert meet her at the police station.

"Do you want the real report on what happened?" She asked Bert.

"What do you mean?"

"You've read the official report, but there's much more."

"Yes, we want it." Bert looked at Hap for his agreement.

"Michaela's brother, Matthew, was gunned down in a drive-by shooting in Tucson last year. I assume you knew that."

"Yes," Bert answered. "She told me about him."

"We suspect Lester Shockley was involved, either directly or indirectly. It's likely he hired a hit man from Mexico but we have no way of following up on that. We found no record of employment for Lester, but he lived well. We originally suspect he was involved in drugs, but Juan told us a different story."

"And that was?" Bert asked.

"Juan came to us with a convoluted story. We could make no sense out of it. He kept saying he'd tell us everything he knew if we granted him and his wife immunity. Since we had no idea what he wanted immunity from, we hesitated. When we realized he might provide the only clues to this sordid story, we agreed."

"Did he give you answers?" Bert asked.

"Yes and no. Here is his story. He is married to Lourdes, an illegal immigrant. She has lived in this country for thirty years. Her parents brought her here as a child and she never had papers. She lived with an aunt and uncle, and received an education in our schools. She worked as a domestic after high school until she married Juan. She has been a housewife since their marriage. She and Juan have two children who are U.S. citizens by birth.

"Lester Shockley blackmailed Juan to work for him. Lester needed a driver for a human smuggling ring in Tucson. If Juan refused to work for him, Lester threatened to turn Lourdes in to Immigration. Juan never found out how Lester knew about Lourdes, but he had lived his whole marriage in fear of discovery. So he agreed."

"I assume you mean hauling illegals across the border?" Hap asked.

"Yes, Juan made multiple deliveries a month for nearly two years. His conscience bothered him but he could find no way out and he had no one to talk to. He never told Lourdes what he was doing. Juan is a devoted family man and the thought of separation was too much for him.

"Anyway, we know the place of pickup and de-livery but we have no other information. Juan knows that Lester had partners or bosses—he's not sure which—but he never heard names. He did overhear him talking to a man at the delivery barn one time but he never saw him.

"The barn was on abandoned property. The po-lice found plenty of evidence of recent human habitation, but that's as far as they got. We have no way to investigate the pickup point in Mexico. Juan never knew names of the work crew there. They called each other 'Amigo.'

"I told you I might ask Elena to do some research. Well, the minute I mentioned human smuggling, she was on it. She reported back that Immigration is focusing on the Arizona border for a large op-eration. My contacts confirmed that this group has eluded their efforts. They do believe the or-ganization focuses on Mexicans wanting to cross the border."

"No Central Americans?" Hap asked.

"Apparently not. Elena gave me a whole list, though, of operations around the U.S. who do concentrate on Central Americans. Most of what she emailed were reports of people arrested around the country."

"A long list, unfortunately," Hap said.

"Yes, and you need to talk to her. She read about the sex rings and stories of what happened to many of the children. It upset her."

"I will. Sorry I got you off track. Anything else?"

"Juan confessed everything to his wife after the shooting," Rachel continued.

"Why did he save Michaela?" Bert wanted to know.

"He'd overheard Lester talking to someone about finding a woman and going after her. Lester left and came back a few days later. Then he told Juan to go to South Padre Island to spy on a woman. That was Michaela. He said Lester was getting angrier and crazier all the time. When he left for another trip to the island, he followed him, He said he knew Lester had something in mind and he had to be there to save the woman."

"So what happens to Juan and his wife?" Bert asked.

"Nothing. We made a deal with him. If he'd known enough to ask, he should have included help in getting her legal, but he didn't."

"But you're going to help, aren't you?" Hap smiled.

"I'll do everything I can and I think the police in Tucson will help. Immigration got solid information from Juan and somebody there will help."

"Anything more about Matthew?" As he asked, Bert swore to himself he'd never tell Michaela.

"Nothing definite. Since we think Lester had something to do with his death, we assume Matthew was involved in the smuggling operation, but we have no evidence. Certainly not enough to worry Michaela."

"I don't think she'd want to know," Bert said. "He was her hero, and that's the way she should always remember him."

"Okay, Bert, now I have something to ask you. Michaela saw Matthew die. Did she see the shooter or anyone in the car?"

"Not that she consciously remembers. However, when Lester first came to her door, she was shocked. I think she recognized him but the mind is a funny thing. It was like she knew she'd seen him but didn't know where. Her response was too violent for any casual acquaintance. If you asked her today, though, she'd probably tell you she didn't see the shooter or anyone in the car."

"Shock, Bert. She may never make that connection or her mind may not be able to accept it," Hap said.

"Hap's right. Hopefully this whole incident will fade in time. She'll never forget watching Matthew die, but she might learn to focus on their life together."

"I think she's already beginning that process," Bert said.

"I have one other question," Rachel told Bert.

"Yes?"

"When's the wedding?"

"Too late. It's already happened. We had a private beach wedding last month, but we're still planning the party. I'll put you on the invitation list."

* * *

Betty dressed for the meeting at the museum. As she put on her jewelry her thoughts went back to that night. That's how she'd always refer to it—that night. She still found it hard to believe that Juan almost gave his life to save a woman he didn't know. Even harder for her to believe was her presence of mind. She'd been the one to call 9-1-1 even after she realized he was the man who had followed them. She didn't shrink from taking his hand and comforting him when she thought he was dying. She'd been the person she always wanted to be by taking charge and making things happen.

Betty never thought she would go back to the museum—but now she had accepted a position as the new curator. She looked forward to starting this new chapter in her life. She already was making plans to ask Mick about an exhibit of her photography.

She loved the new friends she'd met through Hap and Gloria. *I know Elena will make her mark on the world as she did on my heart.*

Gloria would meet her at the museum. Betty planned to publicly thank her at her presentation today. After all, Gloria had been the instigator who turned her life around.

* * *

With his wife smiling at his side, Fred accepted an award from the Child Crisis Center of Tucson for the bank's volunteer efforts. He loved his role in the community and lent the bank's name to many outreach programs. After all the photos and interviews, as well as the networking opportunities, he felt the need to count his money again. His wife had driven her own car and he told her he had to stop by the bank on the way home.

His business had been on hold since Lester's death and he was losing thousands of dollars every week. That fool Lester lost it all because he couldn't control his own emotions. That wouldn't happen again. He'd take his time and find the right person to supervise the operation. Someone who had the street smarts and organizational skills that Lester showed before his obsession with Michaela. Although he'd come too close for comfort, Fred felt even more confident that he had the intelligence to control his world.

After all, there would always be illegals wanting in, and government officials wanting to keep them out.